STARRIE

From the World of Ambasadora

Heidi Ruby Miller

DOG STAR BOOKS

Starrie © 2016
by Heidi Ruby Miller

Published by Dog Star Books
Bowie, MD

First Edition

Cover Image: Bradley Sharp
Book Design: Jennifer Barnes

Printed in the United States of America

ISBN: 978-1-935738-79-4

Library of Congress Control Number: 2016930242

www.DogStarBooks.org

For Jason—you give me courage.

ACKNOWLEDGMENTS

Thank you to Jennifer Barnes, Cary Caffrey, Mike Mehalek, Jason Jack Miller, J.L. Gribble, Lieutenant William Huff and my mum, Sharon Ruby for always reading.

Thank you to Bradley Sharp for giving Naela a beautiful and powerful form and for perfectly capturing yet another part of my vast world.

Thank you to Jason Jack Miller for writing this humbling foreword and for being my biggest champion by pushing my creativity further than I could have imagined.

Thank you to Charissa Duff for proving that military women can be kickass, but still feminine.

Thank you to K. Ceres Wright and Tom Connair for playing the roles of Naela and Ben during the first live reading of *Starrie* at World Fantasy 2014.

Thank you to all the readers of the Ambasadora-verse. Your enthusiasm keeps me writing stories in this far-future world.

FOREWORD

Jason Jack Miller

Bono said, "Pop music often tells you everything is OK, while rock music tells you that it's not OK, but you can change it."

Sometimes I feel like a good bit of the science fiction produced by mainstream pop culture doesn't ask much of us, and the entertainment media conglomerates construct their futuristic narratives around some easily digestible themes—environmentalism, cloning and ethics, AI, transparent society, apocalyptic society, post-apocalyptic society, the ravages of technology beyond our control. Which is fine, because they allow a more casual consumer to feel as though they've participated in a much larger conversation about the fringe issues emerging on the periphery of society's collective horizons.

But when the messages become the tropes, we have a problem, and our collective pop culture sensibility skews toward an artificial median that closes more eyes than it opens. The softening of hard SF contributes to a shrinking tolerance for that which is beyond the limits of mainstream comprehension, and modifies the challenge of 'earning' a tough piece of film or literature. Take artificial intelligence, for example. I'm not sure pop culture has yet produced a bigger AI baddie than the HAL 9000. A cold, faceless piece of hardware that scares us because he's truly a reflection of the men who created him. Imagine what HAL could've done with global data networks and social media. I know, right?

And for Millennial readers, 'post-apocalyptic' is almost code for a LORD OF THE FLIES-esque fantasy world with punk aesthetics and cooler weapons. A dark utopia ruled by parentless kids and outcasts where the theme is the genre, and an attempt to manipulate our perceptions of the piece before we even consume it. The new pop reinforces the idea that a human element is always minor compared to action and the world-at-large. It's test-marketed hand-waving that reduces character and relationships to punctuation while ignoring the (sometimes scarier) nuances of love, companionship, and the fear of facing the void of the cosmos alone.

The humanity inherent in Heidi Ruby Miller's novel reminds me so much of what commercial science fiction has forgotten—that we've become so concerned with how technology can drive storytelling that we've forgotten how each advancement creates distance between us and the ones we love. A handheld computer isolates us by quantifying love and pixelating sex and romance. An alien invader brings us together insofar that we unite to create war, and the shared bonds of humanity get relegated to a messy subplot. A relationship between friends is a footnote to the coming apocalypse, demoted to a secondary story line that doesn't detract from cliffhanger commercial breaks. Artificial intelligence becomes the ideal romantic partner, one who is molded by our every insecurity and desire. In the eyes of the protagonist, the AI becomes the perfect lover. One that doesn't argue or make mistakes. A sanitized marriage of flesh and hardware that allows us to reboot it whenever we aren't in the mood. Fantasy for an audience that prefers spaceships over swords.

I think science fiction is at its best when it's like rock music, according to Bono. When it shows us what can go wrong on this crazy little planet (solar system, galaxy, universe, dimension…) and then tells us that facing the big bad will be difficult. Challenging. Heart-breaking and sad. In *Starrie*, Heidi tells us that our emotions are the only thing keeping us together at the edge of known space. It's an astute move, using the gloss of space opera to draw attention to what we really want—a hand that reaches through the darkness to remind us that we are not alone.

Heidi's a true fan. After our first date, she sent me home with *A Wrinkle in Time*, some Arthur C. Clarke, and John Christopher's *The White Mountains*, a book we still talk about to this day. She could quote entire passages from the *G.I. Joe* TV series, and her love of Leatherneck still baffles me. I couldn't go the distance with her for *Farscape* or *Andromeda*, but I tried—and it had nothing to do with Kevin Sorbo—but I did stick out entire seasons of *The X-Files*, *Fringe*, and *Doctor Who* with her. We beat *Halo: Combat Evolved* together after an all-night marathon that ended just before sunrise, and our LAN parties were legendary, epic ordeals involving sixteen people on four TVs in two separate rooms. And this—all of this—is what Heidi puts into her books. She loves what she loves, and won't apologize for it. Nor should she have to.

She has firm ideas about the universe she's created, and they have nothing to do with alien incursions or FTL.

It's the woman at the dock, bidding her partner farewell as he sails off to the New World. It's a man, watching the person he loves on a plasma screen as her ship enters Mars' orbit. It's not a cloned being, built as spare parts for a dying race, it's what that cloned being was meant to represent to those who created it. Hope for an extended life. Love where none existed before. A way to enhance genetic lines when environment and commerce sought to end them.

Science fiction, at its best, is about the reader's future. It's about what the next twenty or two hundred years will mean to us and our children. Most of us will never be a warrior, or conquering hero. But hopefully, most of us will have been, or will want to be, in love. And a future without love is not a future I really want to be a part of.

Heidi shows us a future built on love. A fragile future forged in the need to make sure the human race sees a tomorrow. The best kind of science fiction, because it shows us how we will be a part of that future, and how that is sometimes scary, and we don't always want to talk about it. How a kiss, more than anything else, can alter the universe and everything after.

—Jason Jack Miller, award-winning author of *Hellbender* and the Preston Black books

~~~

Jason Jack Miller knows it's silly to hold onto the Bohemian ideals of literature, music, and love above all else. But he doesn't care. His own adventures paddling wild mountain rivers and playing Nirvana covers for less-than-enthusiastic crowds inspired his Murder Ballads and Whiskey series, published by Raw Dog Screaming Press, including *Hellbender*, Jason's thesis for Seton Hill University's Writing Popular Fiction Graduate Program, where he is now adjunct faculty. The novel won the Arthur J. Rooney Award for Fiction and was a finalist for the Appalachian Writers Association Book of the Year Award. Jason is a member of The Authors Guild, Pennwriters, and International Thriller Writers and lives near Pittsburgh.

STARRIE

1

Freedom.

Ben Anlow squeezed out of the craggy basalt of the old lava tube and into the shadow of Durstal Ki, Tampa Three's second tallest peak. The frigid air crystallized on his nose hairs, but he breathed in the freshness of the night, happy to have this open darkness instead of the oppressive rock that he and his six-member team had traveled under for the past three days.

As he moved for cover among the boulder field halfway up the giant mountain, Char's slender form slid easily out of the diagonal split of rock in his periphery. Her prime, Javi, poked his head through next. He was having a more difficult time of it. Not only was the guy extra tall and broad, even for an Armadan, but his leg was worsening—well, what was left of it. Tackling a giant puma genetically engineered to exterminate any trespassers had its consequences. Of course, if Javi hadn't acted fast, Ben and the others would have lost more than a limb.

All in all, they had been fortunate. Ben rubbed the spot of ink encircling his left wrist for some more luck. The black flame tattoo may not have been what kept him safe during his missions, but he wasn't going to take a chance and alter his routine.

Matt exited last, the team's eternal sweep. They joked that he always knew more about the landscape behind him than in front of him.

Ben switched on his co-com and quietly addressed the men and women tucked in and around the shuttle-craft–sized boulders. He couldn't see any of them.

"Remember, alive and original," he said.

"Alive and original."

"A and O. Copy that."

"Copy, sir."

Ben clicked the co-coms to silent mode. Stavros's sentinels would eventually pick up their com signatures, but Dreadfire Team wouldn't give them any help finding their position. Each of Ben's troopers fanned into formation—battle rifles at the ready with night vision scopes—as they prepared for the steep crags and sheer drop-offs surrounding the mountain fortress.

In their thirty years of service together, these half dozen Armadan men and women had scaled many mountains, blasted into deep reaches of space, hunted down their share of inter-system criminals, and were still going strong.

Sure, there were some horrific moments along the way—Ben had lost track whether he, Auri, or Javi had had more limbs reattached or replaced. Matt had been comatose for six months a few years back. Char nearly bled out during a raid on the Svetz Pods, and Meke had to be quarantined for seven weeks in a radiation detox facility, which according to her wouldn't have been so bad if all her hair hadn't fallen out. For a month afterward, she wore a skull cap like Auri's and called herself his pale little sister.

Any of them could have died or left the team, but decade after decade they all ended up back together. This was family, even to the ones who had amours and children spread across the Intra-Brazial system. Dreadfire Team were siblings in arms, and the only one of thirty Armadan special ops teams to be *alive and original*, thanks to Papa Ben, a nickname he never liked because it made him feel old, and at fifty-one, Ben was still a couple decades shy of mid-life.

He motioned for the left flank to keep to the trees for cover. The tall, fat-trunked pines remained dense until the timberline gave way to a boulder field buffering the highest mountain in the Chumbal Range, Durstal Ki. The sun had a few moments left in the sky to their rear, but Durstal Ki loomed ahead like a black hole, ready to suck them in, never to be seen again.

Like so many women Liu Stavros brought here.

Anger threatened Ben's concentration as he remembered how Mari narrowly escaped that fate. He had no business thinking about the woman over whom his brother had killed a man, the woman David would marry one day. Ben returned to his combat experience to feed these emotions into that furnace inside him that kept his energy up, his mind alert, and his determination resolute.

With none of the heavy Armadan armor to impede their stealth, the men and women of Dreadfire wore a thin body armor that wasn't much more than thermasuit fatigues of blended nylon and flex steel. Body-fitting flat packs carried specially condensed supplies and also served as flak vests. Skull caps rested easily on their heads—the face plates and visors retracted.

The chilled air smelled of spice, giving a false sense of comfort to those minutes just before sunset.

Above the timberline, but just below the squalling ice storms near the peak, Ben glimpsed part of the great fortress. Its shiny silver reflected the surrounding snow and rock. The structure looked like a double-prowed ship or a wintry bird of prey about to strike.

Drone-like security voyeurs peppered the sky—hovering, watching, listening. The insulating cream Ben and his team had covered themselves in should dampen any thermal signatures, but it also held in a fair amount of body heat. For Armadans, who ran hot to begin with, the effect was anything but comfortable. But, it was a hell of a lot better than whatever Stavros's present victim was going through.

When they reached the break in the trees, the troopers dashed for the cover of the boulder field. Ben's boots crunched through the grey and yellow scrub. The closest two voyeurs snapped their telescoped cameras and microphones back into their spheroid casing and plummeted toward Dreadfire's position as though gravity had suddenly given out.

Ben's group dropped among the giant rocks, some as large as an Armadan surface transport. Search beacons flashed from the descending voyeurs. One flew so close to Ben's position he heard the whir/snap of multi-directional sensing devices. He could take out the voyeur, but surprise was Dreadfire's favorite weapon.

Ben looked to Meke, who monitored his position from a boulder several meters up. She held her palm up to indicate he shouldn't move. His nose always itched when he needed to remain motionless—just the way of things. He ignored the maddening impulse to scratch, knowing it would disappear as soon as he was on the move again.

Meke flipped her hand over. All clear.

He removed a collapsible grappler from his flat pack. The grappler's thin line launched two thousand meters into the air to hook a rock underhang just below the eastern prow of Stavros's fortress. With Ben in the lead, Dreadfire Team ascended Durstal Ki, hanging in midair from a piece of cord so thin, he had to concentrate to see it against the limestone and snow backdrop.

The lift was excruciatingly slow. They would be most exposed during this moment—easy pickings for voyeurs and snipers or for an ambush when they reached the underhang. And, it was damn uncomfortable being buffeted by stronger and colder winds the higher they rose.

Ben thought he discerned strains of muffled tunes and human voices. He caught Matt's gaze long enough to confirm the occasional echo of music traveling on the icy wind. A warning to outsiders? Or nonchalance, proof that Stavros felt secure in his compound?

By the time they reached the underhang and activated their boots' crampon extensions, the music flowed freely, almost vibrating through the rock. The quickening tempo and building beat spurred Ben onward as he climbed and reminded him of training exercises and a few of the kill-on-contact missions Dreadfire Team had executed. When face-to-face lethal measures were necessary, it took a bit more pumping up, usually with frenzied music like this.

His crampon slipped. He engaged the co-com and said, "Double time. I think Stavros has a victim up there right now."

"The music," Char said. "I knew it. I say that Order of Abduction just changed to an Order of Execution."

Several affirmations came across the coms, but it was Ben's "Shoot to kill," which resonated in every ear as the com clicked off.

Ben pushed his body up and over the rock underhang faster by abandoning the careful rule of three on, one off. He went for the quicker two and two—a hand and the opposite foot on, then switch. Fast climbing, reckless climbing, climbing to save an innocent. Climbing to punish a killer…which is what he had planned to do all along.

Naela's ears rang as music blasted through the mind minstrel's speakers. The turquoise laser beaming from the parallelogram-shaped minstrel danced in erratic waves over her head and naked torso while the mind-reading machine floated and bobbed near the high ceiling. The leather straps lashing her to the bed sliced into her wrists, her ankles, and her throat with each movement. Crimson stained the white bonds as they soaked up the blood from her worn flesh. She had always hated the smell of wet leather. She hated it more as it mixed with the pungent scent of iron.

Stavros still jumped around the stone bedroom like a dosed-up fragger, screaming and pounding his fist against his head and his chest in repeated rhythm. He was spotlighted in one of the minstrel's mind-scanning beams—the blue green light in contrast to the magenta flames burning in the double row of wall sconces illuminating the perimeter of the spacious boudoir. The heat and the sweat from their bodies made the air thick and humid with the musky spice of Stavros's scentbots. It pervaded every breath she took.

As Stavros mounted the bed, the smell strengthened until she wanted to gag. The music pitched lower with a droning voice superimposed over a whole beat in a minor key. She clenched her teeth in response to the eerie dirge. It reminded her of a death chant she'd heard on a vid when was she was a child. The character had been slashed to bits, fusing the sound with the image permanently in her psyche.

It was appropriate that that memory came forward. She pushed past the sensory bombardment to hear the mind minstrel repeating Stavros's words…*Deep cuts or little slices, you choose.*

With a jerk of his shaky hand, he nicked her abdomen with the blade.

Naela controlled the pain through her breathing by forcing in two more quick breaths after she had filled her lungs. Then she concentrated, working toward the trance, preparing for the *trick* that would save her.

Another cut—this time to her thigh and deeper. She couldn't keep her concentration. Doubt shadowed the back of her mind. With each little slice of Stavros's knife more of the darkness seeped into the illuminated portion of her consciousness.

The *trick* was taking too long.

Maybe that old woman from the desert just outside Palomin Canyon had had a trick of her own, fooling Naela into believing she could manipulate the world around her with only her mind. So much for Naela being a star pupil and mastering the technique so quickly. But that had been without the distraction of a serial rapist and murderer slicing at her abdomen.

She tried one more time for that delicate connection to the Otherside.

Stavros grabbed her chin and shook her head. He jabbed the knife into her bicep. "Scream! I need to hear you scream, bitch."

She did. Only the roar that escaped her lips sent Stavros scrambling up onto his hands and knees to hover over her on the plush bed.

Pressure built behind her eyes as her blood pressure rose and swished through her ears. The adrenaline surge she experienced was far from the kinetic manipulation she'd hoped for, but it provided her with enough power to break one of her leather bonds.

Fuck the old woman's trick.

Naela had something better—twenty years of experience as a killer.

She thrust the edge of her hand into Stavros's throat, knocking him off the bed and sending the knife flopping to the fluffy, white comforter. She scooped up the torture implement, slashed through the remaining straps and stood atop the mattress. She'd gut this pig the old-fashioned way.

Stavros tried to shout for his security detail but managed only a strangled hiss from his damaged windpipe. The effect reverberated through the mind minstrel's speakers as the floating parallelogram focused its turquoise beam on Stavros's struggling form.

He hefted a lamp at Naela. The knife's blade broke from the deflection. She tossed it to the stone floor.

A knife would be too easy anyway.

She unclipped a decorative piece of metal from the seam of her panties. With a twist of her thumb the clip expanded to the width of her middle finger and twice its length. Her heart sped up, relishing what came next. The mind minstrel's beat pounded with the same anticipation.

With a flourishing flick of her wrist, Naela released the coiled wire inside the clip. The wire spun free and ignited with a blue-white glow, snapping to life at her side as the electricity supercharged the three meter filament.

Stavros backpedaled against the wall.

She teasingly snapped the whip back and forth, slicing through the mattress and frame. Wisps of smoke haunted the air and coated her tongue with the tang of singed silk and scorched wood. The sizzles and cracks of electric light flares promised a painful end for Liu Stavros. And the mind minstrel captured it all, including when Naela said, "It makes me happy…that you're going to die this way."

Ready. Set. Boom.

Ben slapped an adhesive grenade onto the electronic lock and stepped back as the incendiary device blew the door from its frame with a loud concussion.

He slipped through the caustic residual smoke and into Stavros's bedroom. The ringing in his ears complemented the frantic squeals and unintelligible screams blasting from the mind minstrel.

What Ben witnessed beyond the fog of smoke and adrenaline stopped him in his tracks, stopped the shriek of the mind minstrel, stopped time, in fact.

Stavros—*pieces* of Stavros—littered the stone floor.

No one moved, except the woman standing half-naked atop the burning bed. With one fluid motion she snapped a retractable electric whip in an arc over her body. The thin wire, burning blue-white with the voltage streaming through its coil, snaked around Stavros's head, severing it from his dismembered torso and sending it rolling along the polished stone to rest at Ben's feet.

She stared back at Ben with the light orange irises that Stavros was known to be so fond of. But she blinked the color away to be replaced with an icy blue.

Pretty sophisticated implants.

Auri, Dreadfire's gadget specialist, was probably in his glory right now at the sight of so much advanced—and illegal—tech.

Then, apparently using the same kind of internal nano-machinery, she darkened her sugary blonde hair to midnight black. That's when Ben's blood ran a little colder. That's when he recognized her—Naela Starrie, the Embassy's most elusive assassin. She had more rumored kills to her name than any other contractor in the system. And she was looking straight at Ben.

"At our backs," Matt shouted.

From Ben's periphery he saw his team snap around to engage the threat, but he kept his rifle trained on the female contractor.

The remnants of the blast rang through Naela's ears as she extinguished the whip and leapt to the floor before disappearing into a crouch behind the bed. She snatched the little tank top Stavros had stripped off her and pulled it on as she dashed for the closet.

Inside she shoved past thousands of hanging outfits and walls of beautifully crafted drawers to the secret door in the back. Her implanted wrist reporter spit out the lock's code—stolen when Stavros's security team first dragged her through this secret hallway from the ballroom on the other side.

As soon as the door seal swished open, the light blinded her. Someone had retracted the huge metal shield walls to expose the insulated windows behind them. Outside, the cold prow of the building stretched silently into the air, like a giant patio on this jagged mountain top. It was almost majestic and tranquil.

Inside was pure pandemonium. The Armadans and contractors blasted away at one another with crackles of cender fire and staccato blasts from battle rifles. The smell of singed hair, sizzled skin, and smoldering wood swirled toward the cathedral ceiling on lazy smoke trails.

There was no way past the firefight.

A concussive explosion sent shards of glass flying past Naela. Her ears popped and a roar of wind rolled through the room. Shrill alarms bleated louder than the rushing air.

One of the gargantuan windows had been breached.

"What the fuck?" came a voice behind her.

Naela spun around to a battle rifle in her face. The Armadan holding it was the one barking orders during her escape. His age said he was a seasoned leader, but right now he was distracted by the chaos. Growing up the way she did, she learned quickly that distractions were just another type of enemy.

She thrust the weapon's short barrel up into his cheek. A cender blast sizzled past from behind them. The Armadan snagged her by the wrist and pulled her out of the way of the next one as he spit out profanities like he was getting paid by the word.

Naela saw the third shot coming from…

…*Efrom?*

A piece of shrapnel hit her leg, but caused little damage. If her cousin was leading this group of contractors, there was no doubt that the Embassy was protecting Stavros. Things had just become more complicated. Worse than distractions and worse even than the Embassy? Family. Naela's in particular.

Using the force of her entire fifty-six kilos, Naela rammed the Armadan through the broken window. The momentum rolled them onto the knife's edge of the prow. She scrambled from on top of him as two female contractors leapt out of the window after them.

Shit.

Ben watched his eye shades tumble over the edge of the prow. They fluttered like a bird down the dizzying escarpment until an updraft at four hundred meters sent them soaring back up and flying over his head, almost nailing one of the contractors running toward him.

He reached for his sidearm, but Naela had apparently grabbed his cender on their way out the window. She was on her knees firing at a ponytailed female, whose hair was as black as Naela's own. In his periphery, Ben caught the telltale motion of the other woman swinging her arm up to fire.

Still lying on his back, he flipped the battle rifle around and fired. In an attempt not to strangle himself with what should have been a breakaway strap, Ben managed only to wing the contractor. But it was enough to spin her around and right into Char's line of sight from inside the ballroom-turned-warzone. One round from Char's rifle dropped the contractor in a heap.

"You're my girl, Char," Ben sent through the co-com.

"Just don't tell Javi that." She disappeared back into the fray.

Ben turned his rifle on Naela and the ponytailed contractor, but they were engaged in such close hand-to-hand combat that he decided against a shot. The slaps and grunts came loud and heavy as the women flew through combative maneuvers that made Ben's head spin.

But, maybe that was from the extreme altitude and cold. Even his thermal suit wasn't keeping the freezing temperatures from stiffening his muscles and hampering his movements. He engaged his face mask, pulled his knife, and lunged toward the ponytail. She was the common enemy…right now.

Before he could get a slash in, Naela pulled his pilfered cender. The other woman kicked it out of Naela's hands, sending them both off-balance and over the edge, while still exchanging blows.

Ben ran after them, stopping short just before the brink. An icy gust nearly pitched him down the two thousand meter sheer promontory. He'd never had an issue with heights, but vertigo threatened as he lay on his stomach with his hands gripping the stone sides in order to peer into the abyss.

Un-fucking-believable.

Crawling up onto a half-meter wide ledge a third of the way down the prow's face were Naela and her opponent.

Ben sprang to his feet, spun his grappler out of his holster, and shot it into the rock at his side. He was on automatic now as he leapt from the edge and plummeted toward the women.

As he closed the distance, the ponytail stumbled, her movements jerky. *So the cold is finally working on her.* But Naela didn't seem to care about the cold—she was actually venting steam like a volcano. Her precision never faltered. She crouched and swept her leg to topple the other contractor and send her sailing off the ledge to her screaming death.

Ben stopped his rappel just in front of Naela, who stood there barefoot and half-dressed. Her bare skin was flush. She breathed heavily and regarded him with a calculated look that had him reconsidering this rescue attempt. He could either bet all his blocks that she'd accept his help or she'd kill him and save herself.

Wouldn't be the first time gambling got me into trouble.

Ben stretched out a gloved hand to her.

She grabbed it immediately, giving his nerves an unwelcome jolt of surprise. Then she reeled him onto the ledge and clasped her arms around his neck as though she'd been waiting for him all along. With one arm around her waist and the other on the grappler controls, he stepped backward off the ledge until they were suspended sixteen hundred meters over a ceiling of clouds. He depressed the retraction button to begin their ascent. A quick look up reassured him as Char and Matt peered over the prow in anticipation.

The grappler line hesitated.

Then Ben and his passenger were in freefall.

He fumbled with the grappler controls, trying to force a full arrest.

Naela's grip was steel on his neck, and she wrapped one leg around his thigh. "Fucking piece of shit!"

Ben's shout had kicked on his co-com, bringing a barrage of voices from his team screaming at him all at once. He ignored the panicked questions and admonishments as he smashed the grappler repeatedly against his hip. Naela had tucked her face into his shoulder for shelter from the wind as they fell through the cloud ceiling. He banged the grappler as hard as he could onto the metal casing of his holstered battle rifle.

The line snapped to a rigid halt.

Naela nearly strangled him to keep from being bucked off. Ben's chest heaved and adrenaline coursed through his limbs.

Then a cender blast scorched the thin grappler line. The last forty meters went by in a blur of stone and sleet.

The fresh snow cushioned their fall, but the impact still knocked the air out of Ben. Rolling over onto his knees, he lowered his head and forced breath back into his lungs. Looking between his legs, he spotted Naela facedown in a body-sized crater of fluffy white snow. She wasn't moving.

He crawled to her and called, "Naela. Can you hear me?"

Removing his glove, he did a quick scan of her vitals with his wrist reporter. Diagnostics scrolled across his palm in glowing blue letters and numerals—except for one glaring red message: *RESPIRATION – 0%*.

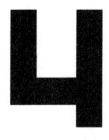

"Regroup." Efrom yelled orders to the three contractors nearest him and spun his hand in the air high above his head to signal those of his security team out of earshot.

The smell of ozone and burnt wiring followed him into the receiving area outside the ballroom where a few servants still ran for the cover of their quarters. Ceiling lights flickered, allowing the wall sconces to strobe their fuchsia luminescence upon the dark grey stone.

The final contractor barely limped through the ballroom's giant double doors before Efrom pressed the manual seal switch hidden behind a holographic painting. From the four corners, the pressurized steel doors snapped together in the middle, trapping the Armadans on the other side.

"Close off the bedrooms on this wing," he told Willa. "Now!"

His mind zipped through memories as he ran for the armory.

Naela. That beautiful bitch.

He'd been warned by his source high in Embassy ranks that his little cousin put in a request for a Writ of Execution with Liu Stavros's name on it. The request had, of course, been denied by those who needed Stavros on the government payroll, yet the man's corpse was already cooling—or more likely freezing—in this highly guarded fortress.

Had the Armadans not seemed as surprised as Efrom's contractors, he would have sworn Naela was working with the Intra-Brazial military.

Regardless of how she'd snuck in, she had certainly departed in the most spectacular of ways. She was still alive, according to the cell tracker he'd managed to shoot into her leg. He admitted a small tremor of excitement watching her dive over the side, still fighting. He would expect no less of his close blood—she was his first cousin, after all, on both sides of the family.

His nostalgia for a time when they were much younger pricked at the back of his mind.

A time when she was mine. Or, rather, when I made her mine. Naela had always been so willful, even as a small girl.

Interesting, the cyclical nature of the Cosmos. Once again Naela's rash morality would be her undoing, but this time he could use it to bring her back to him. Back to the family.

A series of warning gongs sounded throughout the fortress. Efrom forgot his fantasies of blackmail and carnal abuse as a masculine robotic voice echoed down the hallway. *"Solar flare eminent. Estimated Class Four."*

Efrom's hand hovered over the armory door controls. "Get to the tunnels!"

Naela heard her name, muffled and in an accent. Someone was smothering her. She sucked in a choking breath and opened her eyes. Out of reflex her fist came up and knocked her assailant off her.

"Shit!" The same accent.

Naela attempted to roll up into a crouch, but her body was stiff and hurting, making the effort difficult. She stopped struggling as she looked into the barrel of the same rifle held by the same Armadan from Stavros's fortress.

"Don't bother thanking me or anything," he said.

The last few minutes came screaming back at her—as though her head weren't already pounding.

The Armadan suddenly looked up into the sky. "When?"

He must have been communicating through a co-com. Not exactly standard use for the military. Of course this team that just stormed Liu Stavros's mountain hideout weren't standard soldiers.

"That soon? And estimated Class Four?"

Naela ignored the colorful expletives that followed as she pondered the devastation of a Class Four solar flare. An electromagnetic pulse from that kind of critical event could knock out everything in this quadrant of the planet.

She interrupted him. "How long do we have?"

Now *he* ignored *her* and prattled on about an LZ seven kilometers from their current location.

She grasped his forearm to snag his attention and realized he wore a thermal suit, yet her bare hands and arms weren't even registering the cold.

Score one for fragger technology. Those Embassy-hating revolutionaries were certainly pioneering with their illegal inventions.

"That's too far," she said. "The EMP and radiation from the flare will reach us by then. I have a ship less than two kilometers from here."

"Hold on, Char." The Armadan regarded Naela.

"We're wasting time," she said and stood. "You can come with me or you can try to make your landing zone in time. Either way, I'm leaving now." She took three steps before he caught up with her.

"Char, it looks like I got my ride. Move out now and get Javi to a med facility. I'll be in touch about a rendezvous later. Anlow out."

"How much time do we have?" she asked.

"Ten minutes."

Naela let out her own curse as they sprinted toward her ship. She did have a doubt, however. If Xander Chu, the smuggler she paid to get her here and provide her with emergency transport back out again, hadn't upheld his end of their deal....

Then I'll survive just to hunt him down and snap a pair of razor cuffs to his testicles.

Glittering glass mixed with the spindrifts of snow that blew through the demolished ballroom.

"Move out," Char ordered Dreadfire Team.

She gave Javi the once over. Her prime looked like shit. Mottled skin, sweat-soaked hair, but the most obvious sign of his deteriorating condition were his eyes. They looked like he ground sand into them.

Matt helped Javi to his feet. "I swear that puma must have been venomous."

"Something like that," Auri said as he scanned Javi's vitals with his wrist reporter. Part medic, part mech tech, Auri always had a diagnosis at hand. "According to some earlier readings I did, it had modified salivary glands like some shrews and bats and those crazy monkeys near the Archenzon rainforest. The toxic saliva was delivered by channels behind the puma's incisors."

"I always hated cats," Javi croaked, before falling into a body-wracking cough and a case of the shivers that bordered on convulsions.

"Just be quiet for once," Char said. "That's an order." She kept the concern out of her voice, but Javi's small, pained smile said he knew exactly what she was thinking.

"Okay, big guy," Matt said. "This will go faster if you're cargo."

Javi let out a grunt of resignation.

"You did it for the rest of us a dozen times," Char said.

"A and O," came the encouraging call from the other Armadans as Matt hoisted Javi onto his shoulders.

"Meke, take point. Auri can sweep." Char fell into the middle of the group as they moved through the secret closet passageway that Ben had found earlier. If the contractors had cut off their route from Stavros's bedroom, the Armadans would have to navigate the maze of hallways within this fortress to find an egress. Javi didn't have time for them to explore. In fact, they were all trying to beat the clock against that flare.

Meke clicked onto the co-com. *"Clear into the bedroom and into the hallway."*

They just might have the Cosmos on their side this time.

Static interrupted Char's thought. Meke cursed, then, *"Safety door cutting us off this way. We'll need to search the rooms in this wing for another exit."*

"Do it," Char said, glancing at the glowing countdown her wrist reporter had flashed across her palm. Maybe Ben was having better luck.

Naela clicked open the cockpit seal on her "winged egg." Xander Chu was lucky he'd left the small craft just where she'd asked. She crawled inside with the Armadan pushing from behind. "Anlow—"

"Just call me Ben." He folded his long legs into the co-pilot seat and strapped in. His shoulders were so wide they invaded part of her space and offered little room to maneuver.

"Ben, I'm assuming I don't need to give you a flying lesson." Even as she spoke, she prepped the engines, making a final systems check.

A blast hit on Ben's side. The transparent aluminum bloomed into a fractal web, but the window didn't shatter.

"Fuckers." Ben grabbed the gun controls in front of him.

Naela initiated lift-off. The acceleration dulled the thud of the craft's guns even though Ben threw a continuous stream of plasma blasts at the contractor-controlled voyeurs.

"I have to cut power to the guns for an extra boost through these winds," Naela said.

"All yours." Then Ben added, "Three minutes to flare."

"Let's hope it's milder than they predicted." She looked for the mountain outside the windshield, but the snow swirled too wickedly, obfuscating a view in any direction.

The craft shot into the air and thrust them back in their seats. Naela eased the nose up through the clouds. A landscape of undulating crags and ravines fell past on either side of the transparent cockpit screen. The auto alert center highlighted an area in red to the east.

"What's that?" Ben asked.

"Storm alert."

"Just what we needed."

Once they cleared a peak on that side, the storm clouds pushed in, billowing like white and grey sails from those old-fashioned novelty ships for tourists on Carrey Bay. The sky turned white, and the small craft lurched into the squall as it poured off the top of Durstal Ki. Naela fought for more altitude to bypass the incoming weather system.

"What kind of radiation shields does this ship have?" Ben asked.

"Sufficient."

"Even with that spidering crack in the windscreen?"

"I hadn't consid—"

The hologram projected on the windscreen blinked out and the controls went stiff in Naela's hands.

Their world fell silent.

The darkening sky was suddenly illuminated by shimmering waves of pink and green. In the more evolved human part of Naela's brain she reveled as they hung suspended in the beauty of the deadly aurora. But her primal, animalistic urges soon screamed for attention when the craft's nose dipped and they entered freefall. A few loose items rolled forward and bumped into Naela's foot.

"Char," Ben shouted into his co-com. "Matt. Dreadfire Team. Anyone copy?"

Naela attempted to control the pitch of the craft by pulling up on the manual yoke, but snow splatters bloomed against the windscreen as they yawed into the approaching storm.

"Is there a secondary yoke?" Ben said.

"Behind the black panel in front of you." Her conversational tone punctuated the quiet cocooning them. There should have been bleating alarms as systems squawked for power, but there was nothing. Not even the rush of wind singing them to their deaths.

The swirling storm clouds and spitting icy mix parted long enough to show a nearby vertical snow bank on the mountain straight ahead. One wing of the egg clipped the outer edge of the bank. The grazing impact spun the ship away from the mountainside, but directly toward Stavros's prow.

"Aim for that snow field," Ben said. "The flat spot in between the fortress and the mountain."

Naela followed his lead and nudged the still careening ship toward the lightly sloping rock face and its blanket of white. The left lander made contact, bounced, then the right followed suit, then both, sending the craft skipping back into the air.

"We only have so much surface area left," Naela said.

"Then we better make it count."

Naela and he jerked the yokes hard left at the same time, causing the craft to swerve on the next touchdown. They repeated the action to the right, using the change in motion to disrupt their forward momentum. A large boulder loomed ahead. It caught the back of the craft, halting their drunken spin and bringing the nose down with a teeth-crunching impact.

Lights blinked and displays lit up as Char's fingers flew over the dash controls of the *Foxfire*.

"On your six, Matt," Char yelled over her co-com.

A contractor barrage swept over their airborne transport. Matt barely had the shields up in time.

"Strap in!" She had the systems ready for lift off. "We're go."

The mid-size cruiser shot into the air. Char maneuvered the craft at a forty-five degree angle long enough to zip above the mountain range, then leveled it out. "Hold on." She punched the acceleration and threw everyone back into their seats.

The fortress plasma weapons volleyed another round. Char knew there'd be no way they could go for both evasive maneuvers *and* speed. Their shields should hold, but not if they were still within range of the EMP from the inbound solar flare.

The impact rolled over the ship, rocking it from bow to stern, but the extra prutthium rod Ben had insisted the mech techs install on the *Firefox* kept her steady and plowing forward despite the barrage.

"Another round fired," Matt said.

An alarm whined through the cabin, followed by the calm female voice of the ship's automated system. *"Javier Nikevich going into V-tac arrithmia."*

Char's heart dropped. What the hell were Auri and Meke doing to her prime back in the sick bay?

"Impact in ten," Matt counted down. "Nine, eight, seven, six…"

Char, her mind still on Javi struggling for his life, finally noticed Matt had halted his countdown. "What's happening?" she asked.

"We're out of range," he said.

"Of the cannons?"

"And *that*."

She checked the monitor to see the northern hemisphere bathed in pink and green auroras as the flare's radiation hit Tampa Three's atmosphere.

"Just in the nick of time," Matt said, "but you could pretty much pilot a cargo crate out of a black hole and still keep us all within full Armadan regulation."

Her mood lightened, then the medical alarm blared again.

Javi.

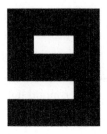

Small sizzles and a few pops escaped the cracked egg and were followed by a series of creaks and groans as Naela and Ben edged away from their crash site.

"Dreadfire, come in." Ben dabbed at the blood streaking down his forehead. "Matt. Char. You read me?" He pulled the communication device out of his ear and tossed it into the snow. "Co-com's dead. My reporter, too." He tapped the silver bracelet circling his wrist. "How about your implants?"

Naela suspected he knew she had more tech in her body than just a reporter. She tried tapping her palm to get a screen. Nothing. Except for a little lump in her wrist, there was no indication that the communicator was even there.

"The flare was strong enough to fry my reporter, too. I don't want to think what that kind of radiation is doing to my cells right now."

Actually, only the tech implants closest to the surface seemed to be affected. As the frigid wind swirled around them in the crash site, Naela was thankful the thermabots hadn't been knocked out of commission.

She would take any Cosmic luck she could get, a very un-contractor trait to be sure. But, Naela was never one to be labeled.

"Do you hear that?" Ben swiveled his head.

"It sounds like running water, steam." She hadn't paid it much mind with the numerous other death gasps from her ship.

"More like fuel dripping onto a damaged manifold...run!"

They barely hit ten meters distance before the shuttle exploded. Her body sailed through the air and landed in a heap next to Ben in the snow.

He sat up. "You okay?"

A series of sharp, quick cracks punctuated his question.

"Avalanche." The word was barely a whisper on Naela's tongue.

They scrambled to their feet, on the run again—this time toward a large, rocky overhang. The sound of snow and rock sliding down the mountainside was deafening. The velocity terrifying. In her subconscious mind she knew they'd never make the hundred meters to safety in time, but she ran as though there were a chance.

The ground suddenly gave way beneath her, then there was nothing but weightlessness.

Does that count as two crash landings in a row?

Ben's face was numb, but just on the left side. He immediately thought stroke, but couldn't discern the tell-tale freezer burnt smell of his brain frying. Tapping on his palm, he tried to consult his reporter to run his vitals. Nothing.

Then it started coming back.

The flare.

The crash.

The avalanche.

Relieved that he could move the rest of his left side freely, Ben touched his face. The thermal mask had been damaged, exposing a small section of his jaw. He was simply numb from the cold.

Naela groaned from his right…somewhere. The crevasse they'd fallen into was pitch black, the hole they'd dropped through having been covered over by the avalanche.

"Naela? Are you all right? Say something so I can find you."

"Nothing's hurting," she said. "But that's probably because the adrenaline is still flooding my system. I'm checking for injuries now. And—"

He paused on his way toward her when she stopped speaking.

"And, what? Keep talking. I haven't found you yet."

"I'm feeling a little…chilled."

Ben laughed and bumped right into her. He steadied her with a hand to her bicep. "A little chilled? The left side of my face feels like its freezer burnt."

"Is that why you're talking funny?"

"Am I?" Ben hadn't noticed a slur to his speech, but maybe—

"Oh, I'm sorry, that's just your Armadan accent."

Ben laughed again, loud and hearty. "Did you just make an inappropriate joke about my heritage?"

"Hmm," was all she said. "But, seriously, this chill is worsening, which means my thermabots are malfunctioning."

"And, clearly you made the wrong clothing selection for executing a rapist and murderer. I might have something in my pack." Ben reached for his flatpack and immediately felt a giant tear on the left side that had voided the bag of its entire contents.

"Fuck!"

"No more pack?"

"Let's think for a minute," Ben said. "The entire Chumbal Range is volcanic. That means we should eventually run into a heat source."

"Unless it's Hephestos's Breath." Naela reminded him that the dominant type of light and energy on Tampa Three was non-heat producing. A weird side effect of the terra-forming process. Scientists were still trying to understand the anomaly in order to use Hephestos's Breath as an energy source.

He snapped his fingers, but the gloves dampened the effect. "Hot springs. We follow the stench. Take a big breath. You smell that? A sort of sulfur, powdery scent?"

"It's coming from behind us," Naela said. "I think."

He could sort of see her now, or at least a darker patch within the darkness that he guessed was her.

"Keep close." He slid his hand down her arm until he held her hand. Sidestepping to his left, he searched with his outstretched arm until finding a smooth, wavy stone wall. "I've got a good feeling about this."

"Are you always so optimistic?"

Her speech was a bit slow. Not exactly a slur, but she was definitely showing signs of hypothermia.

"Hold up." He let go of her hand to strip off the form-fitting thermasuit shirt. Then he peeled off the long sleeved breathable undershirt beneath. He did the same with his pants and tried not to think of the full body chafing that was bound to occur from the stiff nylon and flex steel fabric of the light body armor. At least he still had on shorts. Sharing his clothes, though, was the only option right now if he wanted to keep Naela alive.

"Slip these on." He found her again in the dark. "It doesn't smell great, but it will give you some protection."

"Thank you. Maybe we could rest a moment?"

"No way." His words were muffled by the armor shirt as he slid it over his head. "You're slipping into a hypothermic state, so we need to keep you alert and moving." He gave her one of his gloves, then fumbled for her shoulder and pulled her against him with one arm.

"Sorry. I'd give you both gloves, but I need one to keep my hand from freezing against this cave wall."

"Do you think you can feel your way to the hot springs?"

The slurring was worse.

"Of course," he said in his most cheerful voice and gave her shoulders a reassuring squeeze. Too bad he only half-believed it.

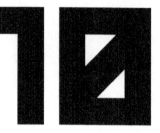

"Keep bearing to the left, Willa."

Efrom lead his contractors through the maze of multi-level utility tunnels under Stavros's fortress. He'd memorized the dozen or so routes years ago, but he was most likely the only one out of the group who had taken the time. The others relied on their wrist reporters and the few hard screen stations built into the stone walls.

According to the last images of the voyeurs monitoring her escape, Naela's craft should have gone down near the tunnels leading to the laboratory. Though every member in Efrom's crew knew their primary duties while at this desolate post were to safeguard that facility, most had never laid eyes on the place.

The group entered the motor pool and ignored the inert conveyances they normally used to traverse these vast passageways. The space sounded hollow without the constant hum of the small electric cars. And without the bright overhead bulbs illuminating the underground garage, the natural emergency lighting subdued the interior as magenta flame ran the perimeter of the room in carved out trenches and clerestory cut outs.

"Beautiful ambience, don't you think so, Tokaki?" he asked.

The female contractor turned her head away from him, obviously feeling as though he had given up a secret about their trysts here. She needn't have worried. He wouldn't ruin a perfectly functioning blackmail scheme with a passing comment. He liked docking her too much. And watching the vids later. When he got tired of her, he'd have his face mixed and painted over with someone he needed to take out of a power position and sell the vids in the underground. Profit and politics all in one.

"Malcolm, get those far gates open," Efrom said. "The manual levers are under the electric lock plates."

When Malcolm made for the dual metal giants immediately to their right, Efrom kicked him in the small of the back so he sprawled face first along the rough stone floor. "I said the far gates. Prynn, Tokaki."

The two women already headed in that direction.

Malcolm pushed to his knees, but Efrom kicked him in the side as he passed, sending the young contractor to kiss the rock once again.

Stavros would have laughed at that.

Of course, the imbecile laughed at pretty much anything. And then dear cousin Naela sliced his head off. A shame. Liu Stavros had been the easiest and most enjoyable assignment that Efrom had ever been given.

Shared proclivities aside, the two men had an understanding. Do whatever you want—and in this the Socialite certainly broadened Efrom's sadistic horizons—but take out insurance to prevent repercussions.

The compromising vids of Tokaki were proof the system worked. She hated him, but valued her rise in the guild ranks more than her pride.

He caught her gaze as he moved past her into the parcel room. Her stoicism was back in place.

A rush of flowing water dampened and fouled the cooled air within the crowded space while reflections of Hephestos's Breath licked at the surface of grey and black capsules resting in launches adjacent to the underground river. That swirling dark mass of sulfur-infused liquid belched its stench up and over the natural stone channel, which funneled it into the depths of this great mountain and flushed it out hundreds of kilometers into the valley below. These flooding empty lava tubes had provided Durstal Ki with the perfect distribution system for its *special* cargo.

And a perfect shortcut to my prize.

Two supply specialists rushed from among the delivery pods, which were nearly the size of the inactive electric cars in the motor pool.

"Contractor Starrie," the tall, skinny specialist greeted him. "What happened to the power?"

"Are we under attack?" the shorter, younger one asked.

"Solar flare." Efrom opened the nearest pod.

This should work.

His attention flitted to two pods leaning against the roughhewn wall of the cavern. The exteriors were charred and flaking. One sported a small series of holes like hot metal had been dripped onto them.

Except it wouldn't be metal in these mountains.

"Does this happen often?" Efrom asked.

"Recently, the lava has intruded into spots along the parcel route," Skinny said. "It hasn't affected our delivery schedule to the outside so much," he was quick to add.

"And to the interior tunnels?"

"Well, you need to under—"

Efrom stood nose to nose with the worker. "You don't tell me what I need. You answer my questions then get back to your shitty job and pretend there's a better life waiting for you somewhere in the sun."

"Yes, sir. The interior route is where these pods came from. All contents were damaged."

"Damaged?"

"Completely destroyed, sir," said the little guy.

"Well, it will serve to make the journey more interesting." Efrom turned to his contractors and said, "Pick a pod. We're going for a ride."

The makeshift changing room on the *Foxfire* smelled of cender-charred hair, sweat, and three-day old cave dirt. It only got worse when Meke stripped her light armor off.

Matt sat in his skivvies and rotated his arms. Not a bad sight.

"Carrying Javi out must have taken its toll," she said, more than a little admiration in her voice.

He groaned each time he moved his right shoulder. A secret smile played over his mouth when he caught her staring at him. "I could use a massage later."

"Couldn't we all." In fact, Meke swore every muscle in her body was twisted and knotted too, but she knew exactly what Matt meant and liked the idea of it.

"Should I leave you two alone?" Auri asked from the entryway.

Shit. When had he become so stealthy? Maybe her detecting skills were off thanks to the new distraction in her life.

"Thought you were with Javi," Meke said, then realized how suspicious and accusatory she sounded. If the others even suspected she and Matt were messing around, it would be even more awkward than when Char and Javi got together all those years back. The entire team had to work through the weirdness for a while. Meke hated weirdness...almost as much as she hated secrets. Yet, she had more than her share of clandestine encounters locked away just waiting to be discovered.

"Char's with him now," Auri said, straightening the navy blue skull cap on his head. A nervous habit the others had observed, but never mentioned, considering they each had their own tics and idiosyncrasies. "What's up with you? Both of you?"

"Pretending not to think about Javi and Ben," Matt covered. "Do you think he made it out?"

"What kind of question is that?" Meke asked. "You know Papa Ben. Of course he did."

"Yeah, A and O, man," Auri said. "A and O."

Char walked in and dropped onto a bench, stifling all chatter.

Matt glanced at Meke, who shook her head—her way of saying, "Just leave it." But, Matt was never one to leave things alone, especially when a friend was involved.

"Javi in the sleep chamber already?" he asked.

Auri smacked him on the back of the head.

"Yeah," Char said without looking at any of them.

It amazed Meke how the woman maintained such a polished, almost regal, presence in the face of each obstacle, especially when the person she cared for most was laid out in a coma just so they could keep him alive. Meke had always had the fondest admiration for their second in command, but this raised Char's status to intergalactic princess as far as Meke was concerned.

"Nanga Ki's only six hundred kilometers—" Matt started.

Char interrupted him as she pulled her boot off. "Can't dock at Nanga Ki. Gotta head for Nanga Pram."

"That's an extra fifteen hundred kilometers," Auri said.

"Closer to sixteen hundred." Char stepped out of her thermasuit and tossed it into the heap with the others. She ran her thumb over the marriage token Javi had given her before their wedding. The button-sized silver pendant hung from her delicate throat and had a stubborn streak of blood through the inset onyx flame at its center. Meke knew Char would have already wiped Javi's matching token clean before putting him in stasis.

"I'm hitting the shower first," she said.

There were no objections. She had more than earned her turn to relax. Only, Meke knew she wouldn't breathe easily again until Javi received medical attention. The venom had progressed through his body slowly, until around the time the flare hit, then the poison had gone into a cellular bloom and washed over Javi's insides. It was as though the radiation from the auroras was feeding the venomous compounds.

When they heard the burst of shower water in the stall, Matt asked Auri, "You think stasis will keep Javi's condition from worsening?"

Meke had been wondering the same thing.

"It's a long shot," he said, "but the only one he has."

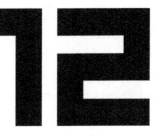

Either she's ignoring me or she's fading fast now.

"How are your legs?" Ben asked again.

Naela grunted. She had become less and less responsive over the last hour.

"You have great legs, you know."

Still nothing. He'd been talking nearly nonstop, trying to keep her awake.

"I'm told mine are pretty nice, too. Maybe I should have been a vid star."

A small chuckle from Naela. Finally, a sign of life.

"You don't believe it?"

"We'll see." The words slipped off her tongue at an alarmingly slow rate.

He hugged her a little tighter and tried to rub some warmth into her arms and back with his free hand.

There came a slight glow from the tunnel now—pink and inconsistent in its intensity. Like a fire. *Hephestos's Breath.*

"Our situation is about to become a little brighter," he said.

Naela gave no response. In fact, she stumbled, and he had to let go of the wall in order to steady her.

"You didn't fall asleep on me, did you? I might take that personally."

Her body went completely limp and started to slide through his arms and down to the floor. He jerked her up and shook her gently, then not so gently.

"Naela, I need you awake. Open your eyes, baby. Let's see those icy blues."

She moaned and attempted to lift her head. He missed what she mumbled and leaned his ear closer to her mouth. "I didn't catch that."

"Don't…call…me…baby."

"Ha! Now I know how to get your attention." He jostled her again to wake her up further. "When we're out of this mess, I think you and I should grab dinner at the Rose of Sharon. It's the classiest place in the Hub with the best views of Carrey Bay."

He thought she grumbled a bit.

The tunnel was light enough now that their bodies cast wan shadows. The pink intensified, staining the stone walls a deep berry, but the real show came from the icy ceiling of the glacier above them. Its deep blue turned bright mauve and illuminated their way.

"Not many people get this view. Not bad for our first date."

No response.

She had slumped again, almost sleepwalking. "Hey, I need you awake. Remember? You smell that sort of rotten egg meets talcum powder scent? That's our hot springs. Just a little farther.

A small utterance was all he could hope for. She didn't disappoint.

Crawling up over a small impediment, carefully dragging Naela with him, Ben fell into the next cavern. He managed to twist around so that Naela landed on top of him.

He looked up at the high ceiling where the mauve had turned to deep violet. "Holy shit. That's something."

Then he coughed as the mineral steam irritated his lungs. Up ahead were perfectly round pockets of hot springs, bubbling like the fluorospa baths at the Foxx House in Latullip's Underground. Lines and compartments of pink flames dotted the perimeter.

"You have to see this."

The form on top of him remained motionless.

"Naela?" He shifted so he could lay her on the stone floor. It was actually giving off radiant heat from the springs. A few drops fell onto his back. This high-ceilinged cavern had its own micro-climate thanks to constant freezing and thawing.

Ben stroked her cheek. It was ice cold. Chances are she would suffer some frostbite damage. He pulled her over to one of the hot springs and tested the water's temperature. Hard to tell without his reporter giving him environmental readings. He hoped it was warm enough to revive her without putting her into shock, but at this point, they didn't have much choice.

He pulled off the gloves and his borrowed shirt, but left her tank top and underwear on. Not usually concerned with modesty among a group of soldiers, he felt compelled to give Naela some dignity.

"What are you doing?" she asked, her words slurred and her eyes still closed.

"Good to have you talking again," he said. "I've got to get your body temperature up before you go hypothermic. We get to bathe together. Don't worry. We'll ease into it. If I warm you up too quickly, your blood pressure will drop and you will die of shock."

He slipped his thermasuit and boots off and ended up in just his skivvies as he lowered himself into the natural tub. No bottom that he could feel. He ducked under, but couldn't open his eyes against the stinging minerals. He stretched out until only his fingertips held onto the tub's lip. Still no bottom, and with his toes extended he had nearly a three meter reach.

Resurfacing, he pushed himself up on the lip and cradled Naela against his chest with one arm. "Do you think you can hold onto me? It will be just like when we were on the grappler together."

She managed a weak clasp around his neck.

He slid into the tub, keeping hold of the side with one arm and Naela with the other. Then he started to count out the seconds so he could warm her up gradually. Her grasp got a little stronger by ten.

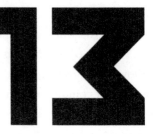

"Enough."

The questions from Efrom's cowardly contractors were unexpected and debasing, especially after his assurances that the capsules were insulated. It was as though the lot of them had never seen a parcel delivery system up close before. Even explaining that it functioned the same way as the giant systems emptying into cargo containers at the Hub from tunnels all around Tampa Four hadn't eased the anxiety. Of course, he'd not known of anyone actually fool enough *to ride* in those particular capsules, but….

"They have an eighty kilometer lead on us," he said. "This shortcut makes up half of that in twenty minutes. Does anyone know how to accomplish that otherwise?"

"But is it safe?" Willa, a particular thorn in his side, asked. She had a bit of an obsession with him after their first time together, which made him lose interest immediately. Unfortunately, *her* interest only increased exponentially the longer he ignored her advances. Pathetic.

"I think we have our first volunteer," Efrom said.

Willa's sister, Ashley, stepped forward. "I'll go first."

Skinny helped her into the river parcel tube. Her face showed no expression as he closed the lid. The seal *snicked* into place, then the simple weight-sensitive mechanism tilted on its fulcrum. The capsule dropped into the narrow river, caught the current, and disappeared under the stone overhang.

Willa scrambled to follow her sister, but Malcolm hesitated once inside his pod.

"Coward," Efrom said before slamming the cover shut and bashing Malcolm's head.

The other contractors heeded the warning and took the plunge without so much as a glance back. Cowardice wasn't a trait any of them would want reported in their breeding lines. Efrom reminded himself of this fact as he climbed into the last capsule. He locked himself in before he could jump back out screaming.

The freefall lasted less than a second before the rush of the current launched the tube into the underground river. With every jostle, Efrom pictured Naela's face. She'd be his after all these years—should have been from the moment he ushered her into womanhood at the tender age of nine.

A jolt threw him against the far side of the parcel. Sweat dripped from his forehead—or was it condensation dropping onto his face? The darkness and constant spin of motion, usually at irregular intervals, played on his sense of space. He became mentally confused, not certain how much time had passed.

Just a minute or two, right?

And, it was sweltering. A sickening remembrance pushed through the haze of his mind—the hot springs. He was traveling into the boiling waters now.

So soon?

Maybe it meant this hellacious ride would be over in another moment.

But down deep he knew that wasn't the case. Down deep Efrom knew he'd miscalculated.

The hot springs were still far away, but the volcanic tubes feeding them were longer than he'd figured. The capsule's vibration pounded into his bones from disjointed angles, never allowing him to anticipate and compensate. He clenched his teeth until his jaw sent shooting pains into his head, yet the chattering increased until he wanted to scream.

The air stifled him. He sucked for breath that wasn't there. The heat decimated the oxygen within the small vessel. He slid around on the sweat-slicked walls without hope of gaining purchase. His shaken stomach forced his gorge to rise.

No.

But it was useless. He heaved and spewed the pasta with garlic and butter from that afternoon. The caustic odor brought on another quick bout of vomiting.

The humiliating situation made him hate Naela with a new ferocity. She was the reason he was here. If it would have been anyone but *her* fleeing from Stavros's bedroom, Efrom would have sent a team after the perpetrator and reported to the Embassy from the comfort of his own suite in the fortress, not much caring if Stavros's murderer escaped. But once Efrom had seen Naela, caught a glimpse of his old obsession, he could not let go of his hope to possess her as he always should have.

This was her fault. Her taunting arrogance had brought him to this point.

The capsule slammed into a tunnel wall, setting off a series of ricocheting hits that sent Efrom's head spinning, even in the darkness. A sudden thought that the capsule could turn sideways and become pinned within the boiling torrent brought about a panic Efrom had never felt in his forty-three years.

He gulped the foul air and whimpered to himself. As he grasped for a new focus, only one came to mind—Naela, humbling her, breaking her, making her cry and beg as she once had. Many times he had hurt her, but this time he'd take pleasure in it instead of trying to soothe her. That beautiful bitch would pay.

He heaved again, just before passing out from the heat.

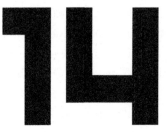

The subtle lapping and warm haze of the hot springs enveloped Naela. She could float here for days, cocooned in the weightless warmth of the water.

"Time to get out," Ben said in her ear as he hoisted her onto the hard stone floor.

He was laying her down, but she pushed against his chest to a sitting position. She shivered, irritated by the abrupt change in temperature, and, truth be told, to the loss of his comforting arm around her. He still held onto her wrist as he looked at his palm. He swept his hand through the air as though trying to find a signal.

"Forgot the flare knocked out my reporter. Can't get an accurate reading on your vitals, but from the feel of your skin and the sluggishness of your pulse, I'd say you'll need another dip soon."

"I don't feel weak." Her slur gave her away.

Ben didn't contradict her. After a few moments he asked, "What kind of tech did you say you were using to keep warm?"

No sense hiding it now. "Thermabots."

"Never heard of them. The Embassy gave you enhancements just to go after Stavros?"

She regarded him with a *tsk tsk.* "You know the Embassy's stance on illegal enhancements. I couldn't even persuade them to give me reconstructive surgery to change my eye color to orange like the other women that had been taken. My contractor commander is a purist who doesn't believe in manipulating the natural state of the body."

"Because if anyone can change or perfect an aspect or two about themselves," Ben said, "then a genetically pristine contractor lineage doesn't mean much in this society."

"Neither would having a class system, in general. Lowers could become Upper Class by the Uppers' own definitions."

"I can never tell the difference anyway."

"Hmmm," she said. "In any case, I was forbidden the alterations, especially since the commander considers my family to have one of those pristine contractor lineages."

"But you managed the thermabots, and I saw your eye color and hair color change," Ben said. "Or was it a personal scarecrow?" His voice held a tinge of intrigue.

"A personal scarecrow?"

"Like the holographic fields some hangers use to keep the birds and potential thieves out by projecting…" He trailed off as she chuckled. "And, you already knew what I was talking about."

"Yes, but I like to hear your accent. It really comes out when you're excited," she said. And the tea smell of his skin was coming out too in the mineral-laden steam from the bath. She found the scent comforting…and arousing. It had to be the thermabots and the water acting as aphrodisiacs. Unless the Armadan's pheromones were just that heightened. She'd never worked closely enough with one to notice. He definitely wouldn't have had pheromone boosters, as Armadans held more disdain for genetic and cosmetic altering than any of the Upper Caste groups.

"I'm more concerned with the fact that *I was right*," he said. "It *is* some type of personal scarecrow, isn't it?"

"A little more high-tech than that, but I suppose the principle is the same."

"So, what's the big deal?" Ben rotated his shoulder as if trying to roll away the stiffness. "It's common knowledge that contractors have little improvements made on a regular basis, legal or not." His smirk dared her to say otherwise.

"Oh, they do. They just deny it, like most Socialites I know."

"You went Underground for the thermabots, didn't you?" Ben asked, more curious than judging.

"A girl never reveals her sources, but let's just say I'm not exactly the type to peruse all those shops on the *surface* of Latullip," she said, trembling a bit.

"Okay, back in. It will be easier with you a little more lively this time." Ben coaxed her over the lip of the natural pool, but still held onto her waist with one arm. "And more fun."

Maybe it was the combination of warm water and warm hands caressing her skin or maybe it was facing death or maybe she was just attracted to this trooper. Whatever the reason, Naela felt an uncommon surge of desire. Her decision to become celibate had been easier than she anticipated. Only occasionally in all those years did she ever get an urge or two. She hadn't even felt a stirring to be with a man until Ben Anlow dove over the side of a mountain to save her. Maybe it's because she didn't often need saving.

The idea of giving into her yearning hovered somewhere between exhilaration and caution. She'd given up sex for a reason—a good one.

But as she concentrated on Ben's forearm hugging her mid-section and his legs occasionally floating against hers, she felt her resolve melt. It annoyed her that she wanted this man so badly she could taste it, or rather him. Actually that was a good idea. If she had just a little taste, then maybe her craving would go away.

"No." She stiffened, realizing she'd said the word aloud.

"What's wrong?" he asked.

"Nothing. Your grip's a little tight."

When he eased his hold, she realized she was indeed weak. He caught her before her head slipped under, then started talking as if to draw attention away from her vulnerable condition—a practice he'd fallen into rather easily since the thermabots fizzled out on her. "How did you get into Stavros's fortress as one of his victims?"

"Xander Chu owed me a favor."

"You trusted Xander Chu to smuggle you in? That piece of shit has more facets than a Deleinean ruby." Sweat formed on Ben's brow, mixing with the water still dripping from his dark hair. She wiped it away with her thumb before she knew what she was doing. Ben's expression went from derision to surprise.

"I take it you've also had dealings with Xander," she said.

"More than my share." His voice was kind of quiet and pitched a little lower now.

"And, yet he still walks around free enough to smuggle me into a crazy man's mountain lair."

"Powerful friends."

"Uh hmm," Naela agreed. "Xander turned evidence against one of his partners in exchange for Embassy immunity."

Ben's brow furrowed again in agitation. "Fucking Embassy. I can't tell you how many times we built strong cases against assholes like Xander Chu and Dale Zapona, only to have the entire case taken out of our hands. It always disappears after that. Let me guess, Xander turned against Liu Stavros, which is why the Embassy finally put out a writ for him."

"No." Naela shifted, her foot grazing his calf and her hip pushing further into his. "It was always known in highest circles about Stavros's appetites, but he was protected. The Embassy would have never issued a writ of any sort for him."

"You went rogue?" Ben asked.

Naela stared as if in a trance at the steam rising from the hot spring. "I'm an assassin. We don't go rogue."

"I'd say the unsanctioned killing of Stavros counts as a rogue action," Ben said.

"You're not a contractor. You don't understand."

"I think it's clear enough that your escapade with the electric whip might get you into trouble with headquarters."

"Once my superiors find out about my actions, they'll issue a Writ of Execution and put a bounty on my head," Naela said. "Family and friends will be lining up to collect."

"What are you talking about? I've seen contractors still in Embassy service do a lot worse and receive only a cuff to the ear—"

"They aren't lifers."

"I thought that was an Embassy rumor," Ben said. "Contractors leave all the time for better pay and less scrutiny. It's well-known the turnover from the guild is pretty high."

"There aren't many of us lifers," Naela said. "Less than ten thousand in the entire system."

"You swore an allegiance that could only be broken by death?" Ben asked. "Why would you do that?"

"To avoid a marriage."

Amazing how a little together time in the tub could loosen her lips so quickly. But Ben Anlow was an Armadan. He didn't travel in her circles, which gave her unburdening an anonymous feel, like she finally got to share her secret.

"What number?" he asked.

"What do you mean?"

"How many times have you been married?"

"I've never been married," she said.

"I thought at your age…I mean, you're what? In your twenties?"

"Thirty-six."

"And most contractors I know were already having their first wedding at sixteen. I guess you don't subscribe to the ideals of 'marry early and marry often.'" Ben repeated the corrupted version of a sacred contractor tenet.

His flippant attitude in the wake of her small confession was hurtful, though he couldn't know the horrible truth leading up to the statement.

Her expression must have given her away because he said, "Sorry. I didn't mean—"

"Yes, you did," Naela said. "I know too well society's prejudices against contractors. Granted, some of the stereotypes might have credence, but that doesn't make the sting of assumption any less potent."

That shut him up.

Yet the looming silence wasn't as satisfying as she had thought.

"I bet you're not left speechless very often," she said.

"Hasn't happened in a while, that's for sure." Then, as if changing the subject, he said, "The Armada sent in a team after Stavros before mine."

"Yes, I know. Their mistake was letting the Embassy in on the mission. The Sovereign led those troopers to their deaths."

"You know this for certain?"

"One of my cousins was assigned to Stavros's defensive squad," Naela said, not expanding on this point further. "It was a senseless slaughter. Regardless of what Armadans think of contractors, there are some of us who still believe in justice and truth. There was no justice that day."

"No, there wasn't. That's why the Armada stretched its influence to go around the Embassy for my mission," Ben said. "You weren't part of our plan."

"No one was ever supposed to know I was there."

"But our showing up—"

"Blew my cover."

He paused, then said, "I have to ask—because we had an entire team—why would you ever risk infiltrating this mountain by yourself? As a victim, no less?"

"Because too many good citizens gave their lives for that woman-hating pig. He deserved to be butchered," Naela said. "And I wanted to be the one to do it."

Though there was venom in her response, Ben grinned wide. "I want to kiss you right now."

She braced herself for him to do it.

Instead he laughed and said, "Don't worry. It was just a figure of speech."

Disappointment flooded her, and she felt foolish succumbing to the involuntary emotion. Irritation welled with her desire. She'd kept these biological needs in check for years. Two decades, in fact, since her last coupling, corrupted as it was. It felt like treason to want this man's touch, anyone's touch. And then to be frustrated that he didn't make good on his words. It was disgraceful.

It has to be his pheromones strengthening in the steam, she rationalized.

She took a deeper breath and caught his scent. That signature Armadan green tea smell mixed with his perspiration and hers trailed just under the mineral notes of the cavern.

Naela felt a flush through her body, but it was more than a wave of embarrassment or physical desire—it was an insane heat, like her insides had ignited. A wave of dizziness struck her. Her vision tunneled and her knees buckled.

"The thermabots."

He pulled her out of the water. Heat seared every nerve ending. She scrambled for the knife she saw sheathed in his discarded pants. She managed a quick cut to her thigh before screaming.

Ben shoved her to the stone floor of the cave, but she thrashed against him, trying to pummel the nanoscopic machines in her blood system into submission. He threw a leg over her torso and pinned her down.

Tears streamed from her eyes, her nose ran, and she felt drool sliding down the side of her mouth. A spasm ran up her spine. Her vision went out, and she suddenly quit struggling. From a foggy part of her overcooked brain, she realized she was going into shock from heat stroke. Her head pounded, but she just lay there.

Even when she felt a slice to her wrist. Heat oozed out with her blood. She thought she heard Ben ask if the bots were self-replicating, but unconsciousness came at her too fast. Deprived of precious oxygenated blood, her mind gave up.

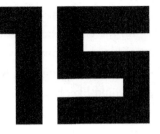

Thank the Cosmos for small mercies.

Ben was grateful Naela had finally passed out. He'd gambled that the slice to her wrist would be a fast enough purge for the thermabots. She had obviously been aiming for her femoral artery with that first attempted cut, but he was afraid she'd bleed out before he could stop it. This kind of exsanguination was steady, but manageable. Hopefully those miniscule pieces of fragger tech weren't self-replicating. If they were, she'd either die from the heat generation or the blood loss. Ben hated to be so helpless.

He grabbed his discarded shirt, which was damp and cool from lying on the stone floor. He bunched it up and held it to her cheeks, her forehead. The cloth heated up almost instantly.

Not enough. Has to be done.

He gripped the knife again and made another cut, this one moving up her arm vertically to open the vein. Blood spurted and gushed from her forearm. His abdominal muscles tightened while he watched the dark rust of Naela's life stain the whitish grey limestone around her. He pressed the back of his hand against her forehead.

Hard to tell.

He touched his forehead to hers and heard her shallow breathing as a quiet wheeze. The spreading puddle of blood reached his knee.

Maybe a little cooler.

He moved swiftly, unlatching his defunct reporter and prying off the back with his knife. He located the thumbnail-sized med foam dispenser patch. Injecting the larger wound first, he hoped there would be enough remaining for the horizontal slash he made across her wrist as well. Ben hadn't replaced the patch since using it after a tussle on an illegal salvage freighter near Deleine. This old low-tech Armadan field technique had saved his life then. He needed it to come through one more time.

The blood flow stopped. He managed to force enough from the dispenser to seal off the cut on her wrist, too. The brilliant white foam crusted and hardened to a sickly orange-pink plaster as it absorbed the last of Naela's blood.

Pressing two fingers to her carotid artery, he checked her pulse. Not as strong as he would like, but given the circumstances, better than he feared. He mopped her forehead again. She looked like a shipwreck victim with her black hair matted against her scalp and shoulders and Ben's cast-off clothing clinging to her sprawled form. Yet, she seemed peaceful and very beautiful.

He had never put much stock in contractor beauty—too calculated from conception and illegally enhanced with extra pheromones so your body made your eyes believe the perfection. And right now, looking at Naela Starrie, a woman who he'd only known through the Media and the occasional intelligence briefing, Ben believed she was the most perfect woman he had ever seen.

His brother, David, would remind Ben that his soft spot for women had gotten him into trouble more times than not.

So why smarten up now?

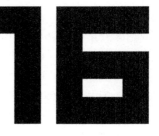

Naela heard her stomach gurgle and complain. She wanted to vomit, but forced deep breaths to dissipate the sensation—she'd already suffered enough humiliation for the day. Or had it been days?

"How long have we been here?" She rose to her elbows and stopped. The swirling of the steam rising from the hot springs mimicked the fuzziness of her vision.

"Hmm?" Ben rolled over next to her and popped open one eye. "Don't know. I fell asleep, too. How are you feeling?" He pressed the back of his hand to her forehead.

She pulled away from his touch and stood. Though the cavernous room nearly turned upside down with her vertigo, she kept a narrow stance and steadied her center of gravity over both legs until the world righted again. Balance training had always been her strong suit, though just thinking about performing any of the advanced acrobatic moves she was so skilled at made her stomach heave.

"I'm good to go." She looked around, noticing several passages lit by the extant pink glow of Hephestos's Breath. "Somewhere. Do you have a guess?"

"I'm feeling good, too. Thanks for asking," he said. "And, don't mention it. You're welcome."

"What are you talking about?" She stepped carefully toward one of the flaming openings in order to see more of her surroundings.

"Saving your life...twice."

She was actually trying to forget she needed his help, so only grunted a *thanks* in response.

"Or for the kiss. Take your pick."

That caught her off guard. "What kiss?"

"Just a little test to make sure you still have all your faculties."

She wasn't used to flirtations. Contractors were more nuanced about showing interest in a partner, maybe because the affection aspect was secondary to status and breeding considerations. Ben's teasing was natural, not full of any expectations or real insinuations.

She'd always craved a bit more fun, but had been too cowardly to try it. She gave the bravest response a lethal assassin such as herself could in this situation. "You find us a way out of here and I'll give you a real kiss."

"Never give me a challenge unless you intend to make good on the prize." He sprang up and started to explore the other side of the cavern.

She had expected surprise from him, not blatant enthusiasm, but it just showed another difference between their cultures—he completely accepted she would be willing to play his game of innuendo. Armadans were interesting. At least, this one was.

A loud "ha" sounded behind her. "You should never gamble with a gambler. I found our way out."

She moved toward the passage with her hand on the cool, damp wall for support. Her gaze moved over the featureless stone, but even with some periphery illumination from the pink fire peeking between a crack farther down the wall, she saw nothing that would help them get their bearings.

"I think you're cheating," she said.

He leaned down with a light touch on her shoulder and guided her stare to where the wall met a column of stalactites. "See that? Someone's been using the springs for energy."

"I don't see—"

Pipes. She discerned their too-round shapes clearly now against the sharper angles of the calcified cave deposits just at the edge of the fading, flickering light.

Ben cleared his throat and tapped his forefinger to his cheek. "I'd like to collect now."

She leaned in, then away in a tease and said, "You haven't saved us yet, Ben Anlow." She left him there and packed her things.

And with Efrom hunting them, finding a way out of this cave would be the easiest task ahead.

"I need to be honest about something." Her tone changed the mood like a Media screen going to grey static. "Efrom, Stavros's security director, is my cousin."

Ben pulled the rest of his clothes on and walked forward as though she hadn't spoken.

"He won't give up," she said.

"Contractors seldom do." He looked over his shoulder at her. The squint to his eyes and slow rhythm of his voice banished the earlier lightness. "Shouldn't being related to this guy earn you some slack?"

"I can't count on the close blood code with Efrom."

"I never understood that," Ben said.

"What?"

"The idea of close blood among contractors."

"It means our bloodline is within one generation, like a sibling or first cousin on both sides of the family."

"Yeah, I know the definition," Ben said. "I just find it…."

"Repulsive? Trust me, the thought of being close to any of my family repulses me. Contractors are more foreign to me than you are."

"Even with my accent?" Ben joked.

"It's enjoyable," she said. "That's why I keep asking you to repeat yourself. I enjoy hearing certain words roll out of your mouth the way they do."

"*Roll* out of my mouth?"

"Just like that. All gravelly and trilling."

"Unlike your smooth, crisp pronunciation." The way Ben watched her mouth made her want to suck her lip—an involuntary response to her attraction.

She spun away from him.

"Good thing we share one universal language." She kept her tone matter-of-fact. "I heard from an old woman in Palomin Canyon that the first groups to passenger the worldships had thousands of languages and variations. Can you imagine the conflict that would cause?"

"Probably why the fraggers are claiming language resurrection," Ben said. "Anything to bring a little chaos to the Intra-Brazial."

"Not all of them are motivated by chaos."

"You seem to be rather familiar with fragger ideals and tech."

She decided it best to keep her covert visits to certain fragger hangouts to herself and simply said, "I like to know as much about my world as possible."

"Like Liu Stavros and his human trafficking? Don't tell me you weren't afraid to be at that psychopath's mercy."

"I'm an assassin, not a shrieking vid harlot playing up to the Oracle Board audience."

"You were tied to a bed with the guy cutting into you."

"Well, I wasn't concerned until my trick didn't work." The reminder had her double tapping her leg with her index finger. A nervous, superstitious habit to restore luck that she couldn't quite break.

"What trick?"

"I don't want to talk about it."

Ben meandered closer to her. "I do. It seems you've got all kinds of tricks. Another fragger specialty?"

"No. A technique I learned at Palomin."

"Were you a special guest of the Sovereign in his towers?"

The insinuation that she might be intimate with Sovereign Simon Prollixer needled her. "No. And, just leave it at that." She pulled ahead of him as though they had never started the conversation.

You never know when to keep your big fucking mouth shut.

He took a stride to come abreast of her again. "Come on. There's nothing you could say that would surprise me. I've seen a lot before you were even in a contractor nursery."

"I judged you to be in your fifties."

She actually flummoxed him. He wasn't sure why it bothered him that she kept mentioning his age. "Don't change the subject," he said to cover his small insecurity. Granted he wasn't even entering the middle of his projected hundred sixty year life cycle, but he wasn't that young anymore either.

"Are you concerned that you're a couple of decades older than me?"

He snorted. "Armadans don't care about the vanity of age. We live well no matter how many planetary rotations we've been through. We're a healthy breed."

"Even when you participate in covert operations high on a remote mountain guarded by a contractor security force?"

"I'm not going to be doing this forever. I'll eventually settle down and have a family." His playful mood receded a bit. "Would have done it already…"

"Except she said no?"

The question rendered him silent.

"Sorry. That was too personal," she said. "I sometimes don't have a feel for boundaries."

"I can tell," he said. "But, no worries. As you've seen, neither do I. The proposal was a whim anyway. I don't lose myself in others so easily." That last bit sounded like it strangled him to say.

"I understand completely. I'm a liar, too."

He didn't say anything, humbled by this unintended glimpse of her vulnerability… and his.

"All accounted for?" Efrom's voice rasped and his throat burned from the leftover acid of his earlier purge.

The contractors either sat against the cave wall and held their slumped heads or cleaned themselves off with water from the hot springs. Efrom wasn't the only one covered in sick from the hellacious journey, which lasted much longer than his twenty minute estimation.

He counted only seven pods.

Clearing the phlegm from his throat, he spoke again. "Who's missing?"

As the group slowly took stock of each other in their vertigo haze and the shadowy tunnel, Willa shouted out, "Ashley. Has anyone seen Ashley?"

"And Mulgru," Malcolm spoke up, though quietly.

Efrom's head cleared enough for him to take a dominant stance once again. "We'll consider them lost." Insulated or not, the temperature inside the parcel had been so intense at times that Efrom feared brain damage himself or worse. "Move—"

"There's one." Willa bolted toward a capsule bobbing in a hot spring farther down the cavern.

Efrom's eyes may not have adjusted to the flickering pink light again, but he could discern a formidable crack running down the outside of the black and grey ceramic.

"Thought those parcels were impervious to most everything," Malcolm said, a new tone, a challenging one, in his voice.

Willa shoved him out of the way and fell to her knees in front of the putrid-smelling basin of boiling water. She plunged her arms in to grab the parcel. Screaming, she scrambled back, throwing her gloves off and frantically attempting to pull her thermal suit over her head.

Malcolm and two others ran to her aid.

"Get her bandaged up," Efrom said. "Then leave her and meet us at the greenhouses. Tokaki, up front with me."

"What about Ashley?" Willa choked out amid the pain.

"She's poached," Efrom said, walking away.

Willa screamed in protest.

Efrom swung around and pulled a knife from its sheath on his thigh. He had it at her throat within a blink. "I'm going to assume the mix of mental and physical agony has temporarily banished your common sense, otherwise you wouldn't be giving up our position." He pressed the blade into her skin, drawing a thin line of blood. "I can make the pain go away faster than those stims Malcolm's holding. And, I promise mine is a more permanent solution. Which will it be?"

Malcolm injected Willa before she could answer.

Efrom stared at him for a moment before withdrawing the weapon.

A final look at Willa reaffirmed his earlier claim. *Pathetic.*

He directed his attention to the others. "Our first duty is to save what we can of the product. Second is to apprehend Naela Starrie."

"And the Armadan?" Tokaki asked.

"I don't care what happens to the Armadan," Efrom said. "But Naela Starrie is my close blood. She will have a voice to explain her actions."

"Could she have been working under a secret writ from the Embassy?" Malcolm asked, rising to his full height, just an inch taller than Efrom.

"And what about that Armadan team?" Tokaki asked. "Were they there with her?"

"Both good questions," Efrom said. "Which is why we take Naela alive." He shoved Malcolm to the side with the palm of his hand as he passed, but held the knife close in case the man decided to challenge him.

He did not.

Tokaki moved arm-to-arm with Efrom as they traversed the sweating cavern. "If the Sovereign—" She lowered her voice. "—or Head Contractor Rainer Varden decided to take out Liu Stavros without informing us, it wouldn't have been an oversight."

"Even the mighty and arrogant Rainer Varden doesn't know about this arrangement. Too busy with the Ambasadora project, as I understand." Efrom couldn't hide the bitter jealousy he harbored for the man. He should have had Rainer's job, but Sovereign Prollixer decided otherwise. Now Efrom froze his balls off on Tampa Three, guarding a psychopath and a bunch of plants. He'd have his day as the system's Head Contractor…unless the Armadan attack was a way to be rid of him as much as it was Stavros.

"I guess we'll know if the order came from the top by how friendly the reinforcements are," Efrom mumbled to himself.

But Tokaki picked up on the comment. "You called for Embassy backup before the flare?"

"It's automatic. If the link com to the fortress goes out, a group is immediately dispatched. They're already headed our way." Efrom's hands patted down his sides as reassurance that his supply of knives were still safe and sound after the parcel trip.

"On second thought," Efrom said loudly to everyone, "take the Armadan alive as well. Some answers are in order."

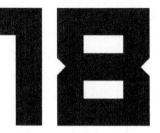

I've always had this thing for brunettes.

As they walked, Ben split his time between watching the nest of pipes running above them and watching the shimmer of Naela's black hair become more purple as it dried. It was thick and straight, just past her shoulders. The color was a striking contrast to her early camouflage of sugar white. Those scarecrow nanobots had probably been fried as well. Fine with him. Unlike his brothers, David and Colin, Ben preferred the dark-haired beauties.

"So, you went with fragger tech?" he said, walking close enough to finger a few strands of her hair. The behavior was pretty bold, even for him. Normally, he had a good sense of personal space, but Naela just seemed to pull him into her. He dropped his hand and put a little distance between them before she knocked him out. "That turned out really good for you...until the thermabots malfunctioned."

"I'm not sure they were meant to be seeped in a hot spring." Her voice sounded stronger, its low lilt almost purring through him. "Fragger technology is often cutting edge. Many of those anti-Embassy militants are rather intelligent. I've studied quite a bit of their illegal devices and coding. Very sophisticated. Almost artful at times."

"Do I hear grudging respect or outright admiration?" he asked.

"Respect. They play by their own rules, which might sound enticing, but is actually their greatest foible. Societal breakdown and anarchy doesn't make for a healthy population any more than over-regulation. I'm more about moderation and balance."

"That all sounds good, but I think you're actually drawn to the taboo. And, fraggers are probably the ultimate forbidden."

"Have you met any fraggers?"

"I may have stumbled across one or two." *Or thirty or forty.*

"Hmm. What exactly do you do for the Armada, Ben Anlow?"

"What exactly do you do for the Embassy, Naela Starrie?"

"You haven't figured that out already?"

"From seeing you standing on top of a burning bed, half-naked and taking Liu Stavros's head off with a retractable whip? I thought you were a beautiful, crazy, extremely dangerous woman," Ben said. "But I wouldn't want to make any rash assumptions."

"Very diplomatic of you. First impressions aren't always true impressions," she said.

Ben kept vigil on the pipes again now that the tunnel floor rose in a slight incline. "Funny you should say that, considering you judged me by that really bad joke I made about your cultural traditions." He looked down at her and whispered, "Sorry."

"Don't worry. That wasn't my first impression of you."

"Oh, yeah? I'm almost afraid to hear it."

"I noticed you like to show off your arms," she said.

"My arms?" He hoped her teasing meant she was relaxing. "You mean this?" He pounded on the body armor vest that ended just at his biceps. "New fashion statement. Not so comfortable without a shirt, but—" He flexed his muscles. "It does make me feel kind of powerful. Actually, I always thought it would be awesome to rip open the seams of a shirt just from the sheer force of my upper body strength like they do on the vids. Used to practice when I was a kid. Went through a lot of my brothers' shirts."

Naela smiled.

"My jokes are better when they're self-deprecating, aren't they?"

"I'm seeing that you're mostly harmless, and I have a personal affinity to good-natured people," Naela said. "Mainly because I know very few."

"Does that mean you're starting to like me, Naela?" he asked in a teasing voice.

"I'm still deciding."

"Lucky for me, I have a ton of bad jokes just like that one. I'll win you over. You'll see." And, deep down he really hoped he could.

"But, first," he said, coming to a stop when he focused on the way ahead. "We've got a few rocks to clear."

Judging by the size of the cave-in blocking their passage, *few* wasn't being quite generous enough.

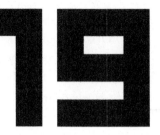

The trauma team rushed Javi off the *Foxfire* and beelined for a ground transport outside the Harrigut Domes terminal, which had a few shiny new pieces patched over the dull and faded structure. It had taken much longer to arrive than Char would have liked, but she could only push the engines on the mid-sized shuttle so far.

On the descent, they had caught a glimpse of the famed Tredificio hundreds of kilometers away and its colorful, sparkling cantilevers built above the waterfall. Harrigut Domes paled in comparison. It mimicked Rushow on Tampa Four, but this smaller Socialite community never had the wealth of their betters so couldn't afford cleanings on a regular basis. Golds sallowed, silvers tarnished, and bronzes greened, emphasizing the outdated beauty of a more hopeful time on this tiny planet.

Char wished the *Argo Defender* had been in range, but though she trusted the medical facilities on an Armadan warship more than anywhere on Tampa Three, especially Harrigut Domes, her prime needed attention now.

Char and Auri were ready to shove into the vehicle with Javi, but a med tech waved them off as he frantically worked over Javi's vitals.

"Sorry, no room. We needed extra equipment."

"Then just her," Auri said.

"No go. Follow Deputy Supervisor Dodlen." The mech tech inclined his head toward an officious man walking their way. A single red rose pinned to his lapel interrupted the monochromatic grey of his tunic suit.

Her wrist buzzed as her reporter came to life. A blue screen spread across her palm and flashed *Welcome to Harrigut Domes Medical Facility.*

"Complete the information on this interface," the mech tech continued, "and we'll guide you to your team member as soon as possible."

"His name's Javier and—"

The med tech slammed the door. The transport shot through an open accessway into the dome and disappeared before Char could say, *he's my prime, so make him better.*

The Socialite official approached them in greeting. "Hello, I'm—"

"Dodlen," Char finished. "Yes, we know." She walked past him.

"*Deputy Supervisor* Dodlen," the young man muttered.

"You Socialites and your titles." Auri laughed in the man's face as he and Char pushed through to the passenger entry doors. "I wish Matt and Meke could have been here to see this guy. I should transmit this back to the *Foxfire*. Matt, Meke, you guys getting this?" Auri said over his reporter.

"They're probably sleeping. Leave them alone, Aurelien." She only used his full name when she was irritated. "You should have stayed behind and had some sack time, too. It's been a long day."

"And, miss all of that?" Auri pointed to a mobile security gate with flashing blue lights waiting immediately inside. Beyond, a high-octane party pulsed to life within a megastructure that was open air all the way to the dome several kilometers above.

"Is this some kind of weird solar flare party?" he asked as a voyeur buzzed them, then flew off to more lavishly dressed guests.

"I wouldn't be surprised," Char said. "When you live in a crappy, remote place like this, you have to find reasons to celebrate so you don't eat a cender. I'm glad the Armadans fresh off the worldships agreed to take Yurai as their homeworld."

As an afterthought she remarked, "Maybe someone knew the terraforming would go bad here."

A voyeur's camera rotated in Char's direction at the Armadan's last words.

"Great. Now the Media will be broadcasting that as a conspiracy theory. Just what the Socialites need—something else to bitch about." Char stepped through the security gate. The lights turned red and an electronic field came to life in front of her, barring her entry.

"Don't move. You aren't authorized to carry weapons Planetside." A pretty-boy contractor drew his cender and pointed it at Char's face.

Shit. In her worry for Javi, she'd forgotten to leave her sidearm in the *Foxfire*.

"Step out and relinquish the cender."

She pulled a fist, ready to punch the guy in his perfect jaw, but Auri grabbed her arm none too gently.

"Don't be stupid," he said. "This doesn't help Javi."

Char bit the inside of her cheek in frustration. Her mouth was so raw at this point that her tongue tasted like iron.

It was getting to her.

All of it.

Javi's grave injuries. The firefight in the ballroom. Losing Ben. Squabbling for a berth here at Nanga Pram. And dressed down by some contractor piece of shit twenty years younger than her.

Auri patted Char on the shoulder as he stepped through the gate and crowded his big form over the wiry contractor. They were all looking for a little blood after the battle with the security force at Stavros's fortress. Maybe it was because this guy may as well as have been one of them. All contractors shared so many physical characteristics—smooth olive skin, blue eyes, dark hair and brows.

Purity might be pretty, but it also makes you a fucking prick.

She decided to play nice, for Javi's benefit, and pulled her cender out of its holster. As she handed it butt first to the contractor, two of his friends sauntered over.

One acted as though he were speaking just to the contractor standing beside him, but spoke loud enough for everyone within ten meters to hear. "Can't blame them for wanting to keep their weapons. Look at the trooper they brought into the med facility. Heard he couldn't even hold off a cat on his own."

"That's it." Char punched the contractor now holding her cender. He may not have been the one commenting, but he'd do.

It was all the invitation Auri needed to throw his own punches and a few kicks. The contractor landed an uppercut to Char's jaw, and she tasted more blood on her tongue. Smiling with a mouth full of red teeth, she yelled, "A and O, assholes," before tackling the man to the ground.

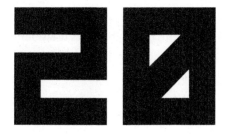

Naela grunted, and her shoulder joint popped as she twisted her head through the opening they'd cleared so far. "I think I can squeeze through this gap."

"Uh," Ben said. "I don't know. Even if you were double-jointed—"

"Which I am."

"—you'd have to break me into a bunch of little pieces before *I'd* get through that crack. Though I would like for you to prove your contortionist abilities."

"We'll move some more rock," she said.

They wedged their hands under a large section of stone and heaved it down the pile together.

"By the way, what did it look like on the other side?" he asked.

"Clear as far as I could see. It continues to slope upward, and there is a bend waiting fifty yards ahead."

"Well, if someone were down here with us, they were bound to have heard the ruckus we're making rolling stones and throwing rocks around." He used his shoulder to lift up on a piece of the caved in ceiling the size of Naela's torso. But judging from Ben's exertion, it must have been three to four times as heavy.

She scrambled on top of the pile to push with her legs. It was sufficient to send the unwieldy chunk sliding toward the tunnel floor. Ben leapt out of the way when another piece of debris caught the edge of the giant rock and spun it back toward him.

"Could have lost a toe from that one," he said.

"It would have been a worthwhile sacrifice," Naela said. "Look."

"Still pretty tight for my liking, but I'm tired of lugging boulders."

Naela popped to the other side without incident. Ben fed her the gear through the opening before finagling the rubble. She hid her smile as his struggles elicited a soliloquy of cursing punctuated by the occasional grunt and groan.

"Let's hope we don't have to do that again," he said.

"Want a drink of warm spring water to quench your thirst?" Naela offered him the emergency bag they'd fashioned from what was left of his flat pack.

He pulled his rifle onto his shoulder and took a swallow. "That's terrible."

"I'll buy you a real drink when we reach civilization to thank you for slitting my wrists."

"Don't mention it," Ben said, leading the way. "I was happy to do it."

"That sounded a bit too sincere—"

"Naela," his voice was low and his rifle was off his shoulder and aimed straight ahead. "I think we've found that path to civilization."

He gestured with the rifle's muzzle to the tunnel floor, tracing in the air a repeating wave pattern where the magenta flames slithered along the base of the smooth walls.

"The lighting scheme has definitely taken on a deliberate aesthetic," Naela said.

They followed the gentle slope around the bend only to find another curve. Bend after bend wound upward, challenging the sore muscles in her calves. The last turn presented a long corridor ahead of them.

As they traveled closer, Naela touched his arm. "There's a door."

Ben brought his scope up. "No markings, so it's hard to say what's behind it."

"Civilization?"

"Or another puma ready to eat our faces off."

"In that case, I'll follow you," she said.

That was easy.

The door swung open with only a little push from Ben. Inside waited a central room triple the size of the *Foxfire*'s airlock. A radial design lit in short pink flames spread across the dark grey ceiling. It reminded him of the Julia Vine, his mother's favorite. Their estate on Yurai had beds of the twisting, flowering foliage.

"Clever use of emergency lighting," he said, following a tendril of each looping design to one of four steel doors situated in a half spoke on the far wall.

Naela sauntered up to the doors directly ahead of them, so Ben went far right. He took in details from the room, including the defunct stationary surveillance stations hanging impotently above each doorway. He glanced behind him to confirm another camera set up above the door they just entered.

"No signs, no identifying marks at all." Naela ran her palm over a door.

"Then it's lady's choice." Ben figured any security measures, even deadly ones, would have been knocked out by the flare.

Naela grasped the handle in front of her and pushed. Then she pulled, tugging at the metal entry several times. "No luck here." She moved onto the next while Ben kept her covered with his rifle.

"Same."

With one hand still laying aside his trigger, Ben tried the handle of the door in front of him. It pulled open with a *click*.

"Wish my luck held like this at Ruby Shore Casino. They built their newest resort with my recent losses."

He peeked inside before entering. "Wow," he said.

"What is it?" Naela was at his side.

"Another corridor."

To his surprise she laughed—not a loud guffaw or even a hearty chuckle, just a small, throaty sound of amusement that suited her reserved demeanor perfectly.

"You're funny, Ben."

"Have to be. I was the third of five boys." He stepped inside.

"Ah. Middle child suits you. As does your name."

"Oh, yeah? How's that?"

"Simple, reliable, attention seeking," she said.

"You got all of that from three letters?" he asked.

"Actually, I got all of that from you saving my life. Twice. Why did you do it?"

He was taken aback. *Is she serious?*

"What do you mean why did I do it? You would have died. And you could have killed me back at Stavros's. Instead you beat my ass in front of my team. I'm not sure that wasn't worse." Ben talked as he took in the darkened overhead lights hiding just behind the cold volcanic flames of Hephestos's Breath that were flickering from more arabesque designs flowing along the ceiling.

"I hope this leads to a kitchen," Naela said.

"Roger that. My blood sugar hit bottom a few hours back. That's why I'm a little edgy."

"This is what you call edgy?"

"Yeah, normally I'm a lot more charming."

"I can't tell if you're full of yourself or believe that secretly life is all just a big joke."

"I have been reprimanded for my inappropriate humor, by both the Armada and my mother, but it's probably more a defense mechanism."

"Let me guess," she said. "You've seen too many atrocities in your half a century to ever really forget them. Wisecracks help to push those memories further back."

"We'll wait until our second date to compare traumatizing stories. Door ahead."

They slowed their pace, on alert.

"Looks like a pressure seal." Ben flipped his rifle around and slammed the butt into the uppermost hinge assembly. Two more hits and the *whoosh* of a broken seal blasted back at them.

"Wow," Ben said for the second time.

"Let me guess. Another corridor." Naela stepped inside with him, then froze in place.

"Definitely not," Ben said before letting out a low whistle.

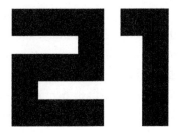

The contractors marched Char and Auri along the outskirts of a ceremonial stage in the middle of the open square. A halo of floating Media screens projected from above the proceedings. Each visual was different, showing the elite of Harrigut Domes society mingling in their finery and sipping on colorful, glowing beverages.

"It's really bright in here." Auri squinted against the harsh gleam.

"Probably the extra interior lighting they have to install because those domes are so filthy," Char said, wishing she could scratch her nose right about now. The electric binders holding her hands behind her back prohibited movement of any kind.

A crescendo of music heralded the main event. Every voyeur in the room focused solely upon a slender, blond woman in a mint green strapless gown waving from the stage.

Scrolling across the bottom of each screen was *Congratulations to Tampa Three's own Ambasadora, Nicolette Sjolander.*

Auri whistled. "It's actually kind of pretty, once you make it past that terminal."

"Just your type of scenery," Char said. "Oh, wait. Now that's interesting."

A close up from the voyeurs' cameras revealed purple glowing lights dotting the ambasadora's right arm.

"Or disturbing," she said upon reflection. "I guess this whole ambasadora project the Sovereign got up is just to find out who the prettiest girls in the system are." She snickered until remembering how she had been voted most beautiful in her class at the Armadan academy during an unofficial campus poll—and how Javi had kept aloof for months because it had intimidated him.

Worried thoughts of her prime hit her harder than she would ever let on. Being in charge during Ben's absence made her appreciate how solid Dreadfire's leader really was. In fact, she'd never seen him rattled.

Pissed, yes. Frustrated, sometimes.

But in thirty years he'd never strayed into that Armadan berserker territory that no one talked much about. After the beating she had just given that pretty boy contractor, she swore she'd somehow switched on those phantom aggressor genes they'd always told stories about.

She would ask Ben about that one day…if she wasn't going to be locked up for a while, and if he made it back.

As their group entered the security building and left the festivities behind, Char's confidence waivered ever so slightly. Mustering her commanding voice, she asked as politely, but assertively, as possible, "May I see my prime, the trooper in the med facility? Before you process me?"

The contractor leading her—one who showed up later to help break up the brawl—didn't even stop. "Why should I?" the woman said, only a hint of emotion in her voice. "The contractor you attacked at the security gate was *my* prime." She pulled Char's hair, twisting her neck backward so their faces were mere centimeters apart. "And, who says you're going to processing?"

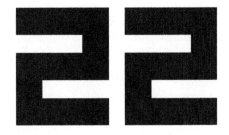

Paradise on a mountaintop.

Ben took in the huge expanse of metal flower beds hanging from a nine meter-high ceiling and stretching as far as the eye could see within this warehouse-sized space.

"Some kind of greenhouse?"

"Looks like it," Naela said, her face awash in purple light.

"And, feels like it." Ben scanned the closest wall for a heat source.

"Maybe my fingers will finally warm up."

They edged closer to the suspended gardens. Metal utility tracking ran along the ceiling where automated gardeners no doubt zipped around and tended the crops when the power was on. Now the boxed metal giants hung inert, suspended above their charges in impotent splendor.

Ben didn't like how the harsh glow of the plants left him blind in his periphery. Naela seemed more concerned with the flora than an ambush, however.

"I guess even tough girls like flowers," he said. "I know my mum does."

"I happen to enjoy flowers, especially tulips, but whoever is growing these bromeliads isn't interested in plants."

"What do you mean?"

"Take a look." She waved him over to the hanging bed. "This facility is growing bio-lights."

"What are bio-lights? Some kind of weapon?" Ben watched the tiny purple creatures squirming and glowing at the bottoms of the bromeliad cups.

"Hardly. These crustaceans, *proto-shrimp*, are what the Embassy grafted under the ambasadoras' dermis. I guess you haven't seen any Media feeds recently. Those exclusive intra-tattoos are the latest luxury fad."

"What the...?" Ben had heard of some outrageous beautification trends, but this had to be the oddest. He scratched his arms just thinking about the slippery critters taking up residence under his skin. "Why would anyone want those things inside them?"

Naela ran a finger around the black flame tattoo encircling his wrist. The sensation gave him a chill.

"You wouldn't want living ink if you could get it?" she asked.

"No way. A little dab of color is one thing. Letting a bunch of glowing bugs share your body is cause to be checked into the Embassy psych ward."

"So your prime's name won't be twinkling up and down your arm?"

Her teasing tone always managed to hit him in the right spot, and because that particular spot was well above his belt, it made him feel a little…timid? That was crazy. He was anything but shy.

"I'll just have it branded across my back. As long as it's five letters or less." He touched the metal bed. "Warm. But, I still can't find where the heat is coming from in here. Hephestos's Breath only produces cool flames."

"I don't see any piping from the hot springs." Naela grasped one of the rods connecting the beds to the ceiling. "But, I bet if we could actually see all the way to the top, there would be pipes. Feel this."

The suspension rod was noticeably warmer on Ben's hand. He tapped his palm to consult his reporter for a temperature reading. He swore when he got no response. "I didn't realize how dependent I'd become on my tech." His stomach growled. "These things edible?"

He watched the proto-shrimp slither around in the bromeliad water cups, then looked at Naela. Her wrinkled nose mirrored his revulsion.

"Though, it may come to it at some point," she said. "Maybe there are other crops."

"Or a vending machine," Ben said.

Staying to the perimeter where the floor was lit by the low flicker of "emergency" pink flames, they made their way around the greenhouse.

"I wonder if Archenzon looks like this at night," Naela said.

"You mean like a creepy purple-glowing jungle? It's close."

"You've been to the Archenzon Forest? It's off limits, even for Armadans."

"Stavros's fortress was off limits, too," Ben said. "Yet that's just where I found you. Topless, I might add."

"And holding an electronic whip. Don't forget that part."

"Believe me, I won't any time soon. It was terrifying." It had been pretty unsettling.

"Inspiring terror seems to be a side-effect of my chosen occupation…" Her quip fell flat at the end as she stopped short and put a hand on his arm to pull him back.

He saw it too, a large wall of darkened windows ahead. Flipping the gun's scope up, he hoped he wouldn't see anyone staring back at him.

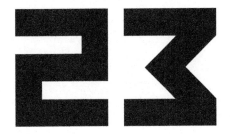

"Tokaki—"

Efrom looked around for his second in command, and found her in a hushed conversation with Malcolm.

This wasn't the first time Efrom had noticed Malcolm in such a situation with members of the team—ever since the incident with Willa at the hot springs. The stench of mutiny swirled in the close air of these tunnels alongside sweat and vomit. And each breath incensed Efrom.

When Malcolm dropped back for a tete-a-tete with Prynn as well, Efrom pulled his knife out of its sheath, but returned it as caution prevailed. If Malcolm had managed to gain the ears of too many in the group, Efrom would lose an outright challenge. Best to feign obliviousness and allow an opportunity to present itself.

His anger rose, but he soared in the strength of it. Battling on two fronts would only sharpen his focus. Unlike the rumors indicated, Armadans weren't the only citizens capable of blood lust.

When Malcolm wandered ahead to catch the advance group, Efrom took a slow look back at Tokaki. She returned his stare blankly.

Still deciding who will brandish the power, are we?

She came abreast of him on her way to the front. Efrom blocked her with his arm. "Pick your sides carefully, Tokaki. You may despise me, but I have dinner with the Sovereign once a month. Who does Malcolm dine with?"

When she didn't answer, he said, "Exactly."

The seed he'd planted might take a little time to grow, but he knew Tokaki's nature well. She wouldn't submit to all his humiliation if she weren't ruled by her ambition.

And, if she won't turn on Malcolm and bring the arrogant traitor to his knees, I'll fuck her with this knife. Either way it gave him something to look forward to.

The scuffle of their feet on the stone floor and an occasional rustle of clothing brushing metal accompanied Naela and Ben as they crouch-walked through the cover of the hanging gardens. The sweet scent of flowers perfumed the air now that they were in the midst of the bromeliads.

Ben's constant vigil of his surroundings made Naela feel lax in her own observation skills—a deadly slip for an assassin. She was too comfortable around him, maybe because he looked everywhere, but seldom at her. Most of the men she knew looked at her *too much*, in ways that made her want to scrub her skin raw—especially her cousin Efrom.

She hoped he had perished in the battle with Ben's Armadan team but knew Efrom was so slimy he could slip out of any situation with most of his skin intact.

Thoughts of her childhood abuser had her picking up a discarded digging trowel to use as a weapon.

"I'll kick the door in," Ben said, "and let you and your gardening tool take care of whoever's inside."

His boyish attitude endeared him to her. The juxtaposition of such a physically powerful man and obviously seasoned soldier with a keen sense of humor intrigued her.

"I've done worse with only my bare hands."

"After what I saw in that bedroom," he whispered, "you don't have to convince me. But, why don't you humor me and my Armadan-issued knife, and let us go first." He pulled the large knife from its sheath around his leg.

"Sure. I owe you anyway. Consider this my debt paid in full."

The corners of his mouth and eyes crinkled like they were used to acknowledging mirth. His joviality seemed a gift from a happy childhood. She envied him.

Then his focus was solely on the door in front of them. They had avoided the windows as best they could, but someone could have seen them when they first entered the greenhouse.

"Now." Ben rushed the glass door and threw all his weight behind his shoulder to crash through. Naela dove through after him and catapulted over him as he rolled to his feet. They landed side by side in very different defensive postures. Ben crouched with the blade in front of his face, ready to slice while his other hand fisted in front of his belly as a block. Naela stood at her full height, one leg anchored behind her so her body was twisted to the side with the garden trowel like a short sword at the end of her extended arm.

But it was all for naught. The room, as expansive as Stavros's bedroom, though not as well appointed, had an open floor plan, which allowed clear sightlines from the living space into a lab space and....

"There's a kitchen," Naela said. The discovery increased her hunger tenfold. Lowering the trowel, she made for sustenance, aided by the beautiful pink glow of multiple wall sconces.

"Wait." Ben was at her back and pointing to a door she hadn't noticed just to the right of the kitchen entrance.

Bathroom. The only place here to hide. She had her trowel at the ready and pushed the door open fast. It banged against the wall and flew back at her, but she stopped it cold with her shoulder.

"Cozy," she said.

Though void of a hiding caretaker, the room was almost opulent in its fixtures, especially a large bathtub that served as the room's focal point.

Ben stuck his head in. "You can take another bath. I think I saw something in the kitchen."

She tensed again, ready for combat, and rushed after him.

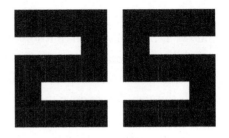

Meke breathed in the soapy scent of Matt's still-damp hair. He hadn't bothered drying off after his shower, not that Meke had given him a choice.

"We're…going…to…have to…take…another shower." Meke's voice pitched high at the end when Matt gave a particularly firm thrust.

She kissed him harder and squeezed his buttocks. He always knew what he was doing. And they had been *doing this* rather frequently the past few weeks. In secret, of course. No need for the rest of Dreadfire to be privy to their R and R activities.

Her reporter buzzed against her wrist.

"I felt that," Matt said in between pants.

"Sorry. Forgot to take it off." She blindly felt for the clasp, but accidentally flipped on an airscreen.

"Shit." She fumbled for the clasp again, but was distracted as Matt hit a rhythm that brought her close to finishing.

Matt's final growl put her over the edge.

He collapsed to the side of her and buried his nose in her neck—his warm breath came strong and fast.

"Ahem."

Meke and Matt both sat up, sidearms in hand from under the pillows and pointed straight ahead…at the forgotten airscreen.

"Auri, what the hell?" Meke asked. "This message didn't register as coming from your reporter."

"Sorry to interrupt." His smirk said it wasn't true. *"It's not my reporter. It's a wall monitor."*

The view pulled back to show a shiny detention facility and several contractors in the background. Auri turned sideways and held up his bound hands.

"We're going to need Colin," he said.

"Think you should tell us what happened?" Matt asked.

"Nah, but Meke should put a shirt on."

She grabbed her frilly pink robe from the floor. "Sit tight. We'll be over as soon as I contact Colin. Let's hope he's nearby." As she cinched her belt, she asked, "Is Char watching this too?"

Meke only ever felt guilty about her behavior in front of Char—the woman was a testimony to professionalism, and Meke hated to disappoint her.

"I'm not really sure where she is." Auri had dropped his voice and brought the shot back in close so only his face showed.

"What?" Matt asked before Meke could.

"They separated us. Won't let me see her." Auri hesitated. *"She accidentally brought a weapon Planetside."*

"Didn't security consider her emotional state?" Meke asked, pulling on a light green skirt.

"Not exactly, which is probably why she decked the guard."

"She hit a guard?" Meke and Matt were both astonished.

"Yeah. And then things just got worse."

"Say no more. On our way." Meke signed off and immediately opened a connection to Colin. "Should we tell Colin about Ben, too? Technically, we haven't been debriefed and Char should be the one to divulge mission information."

"If it were your brother," Matt asked, "wouldn't you want to know?"

"You're right. Regulations, be damned. Now, hand me my shirt."

Most interrogation rooms across the Intra-Brazial were exactly the same—white walls, floor, and ceiling and blinding overhead lights to really make the glare sear into your brain.

And I already have a headache.

"So, what's your name?" Char asked, subtly adjusting her position in the plastic chair in order to have leverage and balance if she needed it. "I thought I heard them call you Francine. Since it's just the two of us, Francine, and I'm guessing things are going to get up close and personal, I figure we should try to be friends."

The contractor's face remained deadpan. "Armadans always joke to cover their anxiety." Francine moved around behind Char.

"Why don't you face me in a fair fight?" Char tried in vain to keep her muscles from tightening up in anticipation.

"Was it fair," the contractor said, "when you attacked James for doing his job?"

"James your prime?"

"He is."

Figures.

"How many other amours do you have?" Char asked.

"Five."

Char felt the cool metal of a blade against her neck and Francine's breath as she whispered, "but James is also my half-brother, so I'm bound to him by close blood. Family is more important than anything."

"Contractors take that ideal to a whole other level, though, don't you think?" Char tensed, waiting for a cut or a puncture, wishing too late that she'd for once kept her sarcastic mouth shut.

Instead, the blade slid down her sweat-soaked back, never slicing into her T-shirt on its way to her bound hands. Francine jammed the blade into the electronic field, short-circuiting the cuffs.

The contractor circled around to face Char as she tossed the cuffs to the ground and rubbed the circulation back into her wrists and hands.

"You wanted a fair fight," Francine said. "Here I am."

Char didn't hesitate. She leapt from the chair and plowed her head into Francine's gut. The contractor bent in half but punched into Char's kidneys as the momentum propelled both women forward into the stucco wall. Francine twisted at the last moment so each of the combatants absorbed the impact with their shoulders.

Hands grabbed Char from behind and pulled her away from Francine, who was being restrained by a male contractor, as well.

"You got to play nice, Francine," he said. "Armadan representation is on its way to deal with the issue."

"What a surprise." She shrugged him off. "Some military. Always hiding behind legality when life gets messy."

"You don't know how many times we saved your sorry ass and the rest of this system," Char said. "And, don't lecture me on legal—"

The male contractor beside Char interrupted. "Because you are the acting officer of this outfit, we granted a goodwill request by your counsel for you to oversee treatment of your trooper in the infirmary, but keep talking and I'll forget all about it while you're sitting in a cell."

Char snapped her mouth shut, opened it again, thought of Javi's face, then took a deep breath before pinching her lips together in a tight smile.

I'm so glad the gardener here was a fucking drunk.

Ben held up four silvery white bottles.

"Is that frost vodka?" Naela asked.

"Ah, a woman who knows her libations."

"Why would anyone want to drink alcohol chemically altered to remain chilled in these frigid mountains?"

"Makes perfect sense to me. I mean, if you can't have Koley's Reserve bourbon, then frost is the next best thing." He gestured behind him to a shelf stuffed with brightly colored receptacles. "Grab a couple of those mugs out of there, and I'll find an opener."

The first stainless steel and synthwood drawer he checked yielded the prize. Popping open a bottle of frost, Ben splashed a generous portion into the glazed blue mugs.

"To truth and justice and retribution." Ben held his mug up in a salute.

Naela clinked hers against his. "And to getting off this mountain alive."

"And…" Ben said before she could take a sip. "To our second date."

"You're pretty presumptuous."

"I'm an optimist, baby."

The first cupboard that Ben checked bore only a disappointing array of useless pots and pans, but the second was like winning the compounding jackpot at Ruby Shores on his favorite machine. "This should make you a happy girl," Ben said. "There's a load of vacuum-packed candy bars in here."

Naela peeked around the door to a cabinet she'd been searching. "Why would that make me happy? They have little nutritional value. This is better." She waggled a can of oil-packed fish in front of him."

"Well, yeah, I'll take one of those too, but these have *sugar* in them." Ben tossed a green- and black-wrapped chocolate bar to her, which she caught deftly with one hand. "Don't tell me you're the only Socialite in the system who doesn't like sugar."

"You see me as a Socialite?"

"Do you really *not* see yourself as one?"

"The term makes my skin crawl." She tossed the candy back to Ben. "And, I don't eat sugar." She moved to the other side of the room and buried her head in more cabinets. Her dismissal stung him. He should have known she'd be touchy about the Socialite remark, but it *was* her true designation within the Upper Caste. He couldn't help it if contractors believed they were a step above regular Socialites, a step above everyone, in fact. Still, he felt the need to correct the slight.

"I'm impressed," he said. "Even I enjoy some sweet goodness sometimes." Though most Armadans had never developed a real taste. "Your willpower is better than mine." He pulled the blade again and punctured the plastic sealed around the candy bar. The scent of chocolate filled the kitchen. He caught Naela glance over from her scavenging.

Now that he had her attention again, he kept right on talking—a trick he'd always used to smooth over the endless tension among four brothers and a little sister. "How did you give up sugar completely?" He sauntered over to her.

She watched his hands unwrap the candy. "I didn't give it up. It was forbidden to me as a child."

Biting into the bar, he leaned against the countertop.

"You're not a little girl anymore. And, besides, this has nuts in it," he said, mouth full. "There's your excuse for nutrition." He held up the other candy bar.

Naela regarded him, her look still hard as the granite counter digging into his lower back. He waved the unopened candy bar in front of her. She ignored it and pulled some vacuum-sealed packages from the cupboard. He felt a bit defeated. Always the peacemaker, he prided himself on resolving conflicts among those around him swiftly and…well, subversively, but as long as the result was harmonious, he'd cheat to achieve it.

He pushed away from the counter, intent on leaving her alone when she surprised him and plucked the treat from his fingers.

The small victory of her taking a bite was almost as exhilarating as emerging from that cave after a week. After such a thorough—and thoroughly miserable—exploration of the place, he was going to petition the Embassy Geologic Survey to name it Dreadfire Cave. Or maybe Cavern of Dirt and Cat Shit.

"Well?" he asked.

"Hmm."

"Knew you'd like it." Ben pulled open the next cupboard.

A blur of motion and a *thunk* to the side of his head knocked him backward and turned the vision in his right eye to a white field of exploding stars.

But out of his good eye he tracked a form bursting from the cabinet and bolting past him. The small man made it all of four long leaps before Naela dropped him with her mug—an arcing waterfall of frost splattered onto the sprawled figure.

Swiping at the blood trickling from his hairline, Ben said, "Maybe we better check the rest of the cabinets before we eat?"

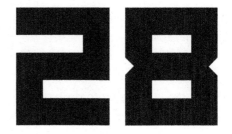

"Contractor Starrie." The voice came from ahead.

Efrom pulled his knives and pushed toward several of his team blocking the way. He kept Malcolm and Tokaki in his periphery as he neared the crowd.

If they were smart, this would be the perfect time to turn on me.

No telltale glances or discreet signaling amongst his contractors. Efrom took in the scene that had halted progress. A jumble of rocks under a gouge in the ceiling spoke of a cavein. The chunks cleared from a narrow opening spoke of a recent passage. There was something else.

"What's that smell?" Tokaki asked. "It smells like shit."

As Efrom scraped the sole of his boot on a jutting rock, he contemplated this new problem.

"I think half of us stepped in it," Malcolm said. "I just did."

Or perhaps it is a solution.

"Move through," Efrom said. "The scat is old. Whatever left it is long gone."

Subtly, he slowed their pace and took the occasional strategic glance behind him. Listening, watching the shadows until he was certain that they were being hunted. He could just make out the ear tufts on one of Mayfield's pets. The caretaker certainly had a penchant for animal husbandry…and gene modification. It was a secret Efrom kept for the crazy loon because it served both their purposes. Plus, the knowledge made for easy blackmailing.

"Malcolm, sweep," Efrom said. "Tokaki and I need to check ahead."

Too late.

A snarl spun the remaining three contractors around to face a puma double the normal size. Its overdeveloped jaws sent adrenaline racing through Efrom.

Efrom grabbed Malcolm in a headlock and used him as a shield. "You certainly did *step in it.*" He sliced Malcolm's thigh open and threw him to the ground.

87

Tokaki dove to help him, but Efrom seized her arm and said, "Time to pick that side, Tokaki."

The genetically modified animal lunged. Efrom slipped through the opening, knocking his head against the rock in his haste. Tokaki froze at Malcolm's screams, then shoved through into the passageway to join Efrom.

A shrill cry from the beast said Malcolm had scored a stab with his knife. The contractor shoved his arms and head through the hole.

"You must be committed now, Tokaki." Efrom held a blade to her back and gestured with his chin to the struggling Malcolm.

Resignation replaced the uncertainty and disgust in her expression as she stabbed her confidant in his chest.

Malcolm choked and gurgled. The cat had gathered its faculties enough to attack again. A paw the size of a serving platter swiped into the opening above Malcolm's head, landing with a tear of claws across the side of his face. His body convulsed and jerked as the animal fought to pull him back into the passageway with it. Efrom kicked at the stones braced above the cleared section until one slid loose. It toppled onto Malcolm's back with a crack, jamming the man's body into the opening and blocking the lion's passage.

Blood poured from Malcolm's open mouth, but his eyes had not yet glazed over in death when the crunching sounds began.

"At least the poor thing will have something to eat," Efrom said.

Tokaki vomited.

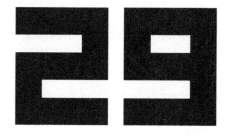

Pathetic little moans escaped their unexpected visitor's semi-conscious form as Naela cinched the last knot binding his leg to the wooden chair. No doubt he was the caretaker of this outpost, so it may have been adding insult to injury by using shredded bits of the man's own clothing from the closet as his restraints. Though Ben would no doubt consider the affront nothing compared to the goose egg rising on his bruised head.

"So, how long do you think this fucker was twisted up like a pretzel in that cupboard?" he asked.

"Could have been from the time we broke into the greenhouse."

"I don't know. He was pretty spry when he heaved that jar of jam at me and bolted for the door."

"I've been contorted in tighter places than that for extended periods of time. Though it takes constant muscle manipulation to maintain flexibility."

"I'm going to ignore everything you just said, otherwise my mouth is going to get me into trouble," Ben said.

Naela didn't have time to respond to his innuendo because the caretaker let out a giant, angry groan and bobbed his head on his chest.

"Finally," Ben said. "I actually thought you killed this asshole with that mug of frost. Good aim, by the way."

The caretaker blubbered and squawked and blinked his eyes at Ben. "Armadan." He pulled in a sharp intake of breath. "Oh no, oh no, oh no."

The guy's expression morphed into a mix of surprise and alarm with a rictus smile Ben had only seen on lesser primates, and the man's voice took on a high-pitched kind of squeal as he spoke…in really fast bursts.

"What the fuck, who are you, what are you doing here, what did you do to me?" He tugged at his bindings, but only managed to squirm and rock the chair on the stone floor.

"He's in the middle of a narcotic slide," Naela said.

The caretaker stopped struggling to stare at Naela. When he didn't move or even blink for half a minute, Naela walked over and snapped her fingers in his face.

He bit the air around her. "I want a taste. Contractor bitches taste good." He looked over at Ben. Drool flowed freely down the side of the caretaker's mouth. "You taste her yet? She taste good? She looks good. Good enough to—"

Ben slapped the man across the face before Naela could.

Chivalrous.

Nothing happened at first, then the man renewed his rocking and added some high-pitched wails to the show.

"Buddy, calm down," Ben said, but the guy showed no sign of hearing him.

Shouting, Ben asked, "What's your name?" To Naela, he said, "He's not sliding. He's already slid. Right off the Chumbal Range, out of Tampa Three's orbit, and heading for Deleine way at the end of the system."

"We'll have to wait until the drugs wear off before we can get anything out of him."

"Maybe, but I can't listen to this shrieking all night...or all day. I don't even know what the hell time it is."

"Mayfield. Sixteen hundred hours, forty-two minutes," the caretaker said, then flashed that weird smile that practically showed all the teeth in his mouth.

Naela shared a look with Ben.

"Is Mayfield your name?" she asked.

"Mayfield," he screamed and giggled-hiccuped, then recited the time again—allowing for the change in minutes.

"How could you possibly know that?" Ben asked.

"Been counting. Counting. All day. All night. Counting," Mayfield screamed and rocked in his chair until it tipped over. His shoulder smacked the stone just before his head did. Still he didn't stop his swaying. Each motion ended with Mayfield's head bouncing off the floor and a monkey grin.

"Are you kidding me?" Ben picked Mayfield up, chair and all, and carried him into the greenhouse. He put both hands on the chair arms and leaned in close.

"I'd back up," Naela warned from her spot leaning against the door jamb.

Mayfield sucked in his saliva. Ben pushed away from the little man before the pathetic stream of spittle could douse him. With an ongoing giggle, Mayfield spouted off the time again. Ben pointed a finger at him, opened his mouth to say something, then simply closed it, and joined Naela back in the kitchen.

"I think you made a new friend," she said.

Ben grabbed a vacuum-packed meal and sat down at the table. As he ripped open the seal on the Cosmos-knew-what and scooped in a mouthful of brown gelatinous protein, he said, "You're the one he wanted to taste."

The soft glow of yellow lamps and recessed lighting blended calmly with the backlit glow of medical monitors here in Javi's hospital suite. The only detriment to the healing mood of the room was the condescending Socialite doctor prattling on as he checked her prime's vitals.

Char clasped her hands behind her back so she wouldn't be tempted to smack—what was his name? Polter? Poley? No matter, she was calling him Doctor Pissy in her mind because he made it known many times that he wasn't on call right now and that he was missing the Ambasadora ceremony.

Well, he had met his match in Char today.

It probably wasn't often the guy brought out his tunic suit, judging by its tight fit and outmoded embroidery along the side zip.

And what color is that exactly? Pea green or neon puke?

His hand glowed blue. He flipped it over to read the message scrolling across his palm from his wrist reporter. "Finally we have the Armadan's toxicological screen."

"His name is Javier." Char's jaw was clenched so tightly she nearly broke a tooth. "Or Trooper Nikevich."

"Does Trooper Nikevich use recreational drugs?" the doctor asked.

"No."

"Not even stims…or alcohol?" Doctor Pissy's voice said he wouldn't believe another no, because after all, weren't all Armadans alcoholics and stim abusers?

Char hated the words she was about to say, but Javi's care depended on the truth. "Occasional use of both in the field."

"And off duty?"

"Seldom."

"Recently?"

"Why the hell does it matter?"

"No need for the attitude. His symptoms—bloodshot eyes, confusion, fatigue, difficulty breathing—are all congruent with a poison we see in a particular group of synthesized drugs. When mixed with certain stimulants and ingested, the combination offers a heightened sensory experience. Much of the poison gets filtered through the liver and is relatively harmless."

"This doesn't look harmless to me."

"If you would allow me to finish. Given the Arm—*Trooper Nikevich's* light sensitivity, severe headache, shaking and loss of consciousness, his reaction is severe. I suspect it's because the poison was an exceptionally high dose and went directly into his bloodstream via the wound."

He looked over at her, eyes squinted. "You say he was attacked by a puma."

"Yes, a genetically enhanced puma with venom glands and fangs."

"That would be highly illegal—"

"You bet your ass it's fucking illegal, but that doesn't change the fact that it was there and that it sunk its illegal teeth into my prime. So, do you have an anti-venom?"

"It's actually a poison."

"Can you save him?" she screamed.

He cleared his throat and smoothed his lapel over his pudgy belly. "Yes, thanks to our timely treatment, otherwise he would have died."

"So, he's all right?" Char didn't even care about the derisive tone.

"Once he sleeps it off and the rest of the poison filters out of his system, then yes. If you have any other questions the nurse will entertain them." Doctor Pissy walked out of the room without a good-bye.

As soon as the door closed, Char went to Javi's bedside, cradled his hand to her face, and wept.

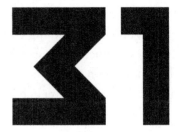

Best dreams I've had in a while.

Though Ben was accosted all night by Naela's sweet scent on the pillow, he was glad he'd insisted that she rest first. He was smelling better himself. His freshly laundered clothes smelled exactly like the lavender soap he'd used in the tub and the sheets on Mayfield's bed...and Naela.

His first glimpse of her this morning was endearing. Having rummaged through Mayfield's closet, she found a long-sleeved shirt and stiff worker's pants that fit her much better than Ben's hand-me-downs from the tunnel. He admitted to feeling much happier fully clothed again...and clean.

"Did you sleep well?" Naela handed him a mug of juice. Her raised brow said he must not look like it.

"Yeah," he said, feeling unusually self-conscious. "Lots of dreams, but, you know." He swallowed the juice in one gulp.

"You still look haggard."

"Thank you for the boost in confidence."

"Sorry, I meant you appear tired."

"I just haven't shaved in a while." In truth, the fatigue hadn't really left him. He'd catch a long nap once they were off this mountain.

A ruckus from the living room ended with a squeaky, "Hey. Water."

"How *you* feeling, Mayfield?" Ben raised his voice to be heard in the next room.

"Don't ask." Naela poured some water into a mug.

"I take it he's kept you entertained."

"He was asleep until about an hour ago, and I had to threaten his most precious body parts to keep him from screaming and waking you up."

"That was very thoughtful. And to repay the favor..." Ben took the mug from Naela's hand. "...I'll deliver this."

Mayfield made a noise in between a snarl and grunt when Ben approached.

He gave the caretaker a sip of water.

When he tried to gulp the whole glass, Ben pulled it away and said, "You give me some answers and I give you some more water."

"And food," Mayfield said. "I neeeed...sustenance."

"Still got that shrieky voice, huh? I was really hoping that particular idiosyncrasy was a result of the dosing."

"He might yet be sliding," Naela said.

"No," Mayfield yelled. "No more sliding. No more sliding."

"Or he's permanently fried his brain," Ben said. "Ought to be fun getting anything out of him."

"Give me some more. I'll tell you."

Ben held the mug while Mayfield guzzled down the water. "Another."

"Give me an answer first." Ben handed the mug to Naela for refilling. "If you're really good, maybe Naela can be persuaded to offer you some of that expensive chilled vodka you keep on hand."

Mayfield's nose and eyes scrunched up like he was constipated. He groaned and rocked. "No frost," he screamed. "More water."

"Suit yourself," Ben said. "Now, what is this place?"

"My lab."

"Who owns it?" Naela held the mug in front of Mayfield's face. "Not you."

His wide pupils flickered from her to the water as if deciding which he would really prefer. "Someone...someone else."

"No shit," Ben said. "Who?"

He squirmed and rolled his eyes around as if in deliberation, always bringing his gaze to rest again on the mug in Naela's hand. Finally, he blurted out, "The Embassy."

Naela gave the man a drink.

Ben faced away from Mayfield to whisper in Naela's ear, "This isn't good. That means your cousin wasn't acting as a mercenary for Stavros. He's here on behalf of the Sovereign."

"Which means when the flare hit, a rescue team was automatically dispatched," she said.

"Yeah, and probably not for Stavros and the contractors, but for the contents of this garden lab. We might have been safer back at the fortress."

"Food." Mayfield screamed like a child being ignored by the grown-ups.

"This guy is going to have to starve because I am not spoon-feeding him," Ben said.

"Some carbohydrates in his stomach might sober him up," Naela said. "I'll give him back one arm. And, if he tries anything, I'll hit him with my mug again."

Three vacuum-packed meals later, Mayfield calmed down. He even dabbed at his mouth with a napkin when he was finished.

Ben flipped a chair around and sat facing the man with his arms folded across the seatback. "We all done sliding?"

Mayfield pushed a few blobs of stewed carrots around on his tray. "Unless you're willing to give me some more?" His voice retained its shrillness, but at least he spoke in full sentences now.

"Not on your life. I need you coherent so we can establish the situation."

"The *situation* is that you aren't supposed to be here. Contractor Starrie—"

"He means Efrom," Naela said. "Not me."

She didn't need any confusion about her allegiance. Ben barely knew her, and from what she had gathered, he wasn't fond of contractors generally, though he seemed to like her well enough. At least, she wanted him to.

"I kind of figured that," he said.

His light tone made her feel foolish, but relieved.

Mayfield clammed up at the news that another Contractor Starrie stood before him.

Ben continued his interrogation. "You called this a lab. Looks like a greenhouse to me. What do you do here?"

Mayfield wouldn't take his gaze off Naela.

Ben waved a hand into the man's field of vision. "It's rude to ignore a new friend when he's talking to you."

"I'm a bio-chemist. I study endangered plants for medicinal purposes."

"A lab like this," Naela said, "high on a secluded mountain, all by yourself? I'm betting your purposes fall more into the bio-weapons category."

"Like that hollow-toothed puma who venomized one of my troopers?"

Mayfield stiffened. "Why is she here?"

"She's my bodyguard," Ben said. "Are you going to answer my question? You know something about that genetically engineered cat guarding this complex?"

"No," Mayfield said. "Now, answer *my* question. Why is she really here?"

Though not schooled in questioning techniques—most of her targets never lived long enough for a conversation—Naela jumped on the opportunity. "I was sent to kill you."

"By who?"

"Liu Stavros has been making side deals and creating an underground demand for your product."

"I knew it," Mayfield squeaked. "You're a rogue. You have no idea what you stumbled into. Liu was just a face to the outside. He had no deal-making authority. This is an Embassy enterprise." His speech drew out in a smug tone. "The contractors coming for you are from the guild."

"Ooh. *From the guild.*" Ben mocked their prisoner. "I'm terrified."

"Why do you have an Armadan with you? Is he your partner?" Mayfield asked, ignoring Ben this time in deference to the person he believed was truly in charge.

"My *partner* is none of your business," she said. "You should be more concerned with giving us answers." She grabbed him by a tuft of blond hair and pulled his head back. "Because I don't see any other contractors here right now but me."

"You're right. You're right. I was sanctioned by the Embassy for the study of botanical-based weapons using Archenzonian plant species."

"That explains the embargo on the Archenzon Forest," Ben said.

"Do you work here alone?" Naela asked.

"Yes, the facility is usually automated. No one is allowed inside except for Contractor Starrie when he delivers supplies or specific orders. And, even he's not welcome. Not after…."

"After what?" Naela asked. Nothing would surprise her.

"Nothing. I took care of it."

She focused the man by asking, "Did you make the venom for the puma?"

He hesitated, then said with a confidence he couldn't really stand behind, "I work with plants and proto-shrimp, not large predators."

"What do the proto—"

"I have to use the bathroom," Mayfield screamed. "Unless you want me to go right here." A hint of the crazed doser glinted in his eye.

Naela looked at Ben. "I think you can take over again."

"Pry this one open." Efrom stood inside the round passageway where several doors awaited them in a half circle. He pointed to one on his farthest left.

No one moved.

"Must I repeat myself?"

"This door is ajar." Tokaki gestured toward the one leading to the greenhouse.

"Yes, because Naela and the Armadan are heading to the laboratory, but we need provisions first."

Enthused by the thought of food and water, Pablo and Carson made quick work of the hinges. What they found inside perked them up much more.

"It's an armory," Tokaki said.

Efrom stepped inside and lifted a set of handguns from the rack on the wall. With his contractors surrounding him he wondered for just a moment whether arming them with long-range projectile weapons was signing his own Writ of Execution.

"Distribute the weaponry," Efrom said.

Tokaki went about her task, never indicating her mood or intentions.

"Eat and hydrate while you can," he said to the others. "We're nearly upon them."

If it had been one of Efrom's old commanders who pushed the group this hard out of resentment toward a family member, he would have slyly cut the contractor's throat. But, after Malcolm's grisly demise, none of these sheep had it in them to raise a knife toward him. Not even Tokaki.

He'd still watch, though, because killing a man with a distant bullet was much different than face-to-face. Naela was definitely an up close and personal killer. Stavros's dismembered corpse was proof of that.

Maybe it was the assassin training. More likely, it was the thrill of defeating her enemy with her bare hands when given the chance. It would be for Efrom.

The thought of her violent tendencies aroused him. She had fought him so many times during her youth, and if her brother Nikos hadn't returned to claim her as his prime, Efrom would have made sure Naela married him first.

Bore my child first.

Then Nikos and anyone else who wanted her could have their turn, but she would always have to return to Efrom as his prime. In the end, both men lost her to the assassin program, but Efrom still harbored the fantasy of her from time to time. Even after three marriages of his own. Hunting Naela now allowed the fantasy to morph into an obsession.

He caught Tokaki's gaze as she bit off a piece of the tough nutrition bars they'd been eating since leaving the fortress. So far, she was the closest in physical appearance and in spirit to Naela that he had found, but like all the others, including an amour who had to be committed to the Embassy's psychiatric hospital at the Hub, Tokaki was breaking much too easily.

The fact that she hadn't tried to kill him yet proved it.

Like taking care of an evil little, high-strung toddler.

Ben pounded on the bathroom door. "Hey, you still awake?"

"He's been in there a while," Naela said.

A hysterical giggle floated under the door jamb.

"Are you kidding me?" Ben pounded again. "Are you dosing in there?"

"Don't most drug addicts have a hidden cache?" Naela gestured around the plush living area. "He probably has several. We might not even notice stashed droppers or pills if we weren't looking for them."

"Mayfield, if you don't open this door now, I'm going to break it down and drag you out here by your ear." Ben raised his fist to pound once more, but the door clicked open.

Mayfield peeked around the side at Ben and said, "Not working yet. Didn't take enough."

Ben snagged the man by his shirt—he'd changed clothes in the bathroom as well—and hauled him through the door. "Oh, I think you've had plenty."

"Not me." He slapped Ben's hand away and meandered around the space. He avoided the sitting area where Naela stood and paced near the kitchen pantry. He balled and unballed his fists and murmured, "Frost. We need to drink."

"The last thing you need is to mix alcohol with whatever you just took," Ben said.

Mayfield ran over to the counter where the half-empty bottle of vodka waited. He popped off the top and poured a mug to overflowing.

Ben shooed the man away like he used to with the ducks that waddled up onto the deck of his lake house. "We need you coherent."

"Then you drink it," Mayfield screamed at the top of his lungs before bolting for the pantry.

Naela was right behind him. Not like he could get far, but maybe he'd also stashed some weapons as well as drugs.

What a pain in the ass.

Ben shouldered into the narrow doorway, past fully stocked shelves of bulk dry goods, around a corner, and nearly ran into Naela. His head jerked around in the confined space. "Where's—"

"He disappeared," she said.

"What?" Ben knocked boxes of cereal and bags of flour off the nearest shelf. "Be careful. That little shit can squeeze himself into places like a pet octopus escaping its tank."

"He's not here."

"Then where the hell did he go? He didn't get past me out the door. I could barely fit in here." He was feeling a little claustrophobic among the stainless steel shelves and the monochromatic beige of generic labels surrounding him.

"Do you smell that?" Naela asked.

"It wasn't me."

"It smells like…the beach."

Now that Ben was concentrating, he did catch a whiff of fake shore, like an air freshener.

"Here." Naela ran her finger along the wall behind a shelf. "Stand back a bit."

Ben gave her some room. He heard the *click* of a latch disengaging and the shelf pulled away from the wall a few centimeters, perfuming the pantry with a kind of salty coconut scent.

"It's another secret passage," Naela said. "Like the one in Stavros's closet."

"Got your blades on you?" Ben asked.

Naela drew the kitchen knives from her makeshift sheath.

"In we go," he said.

Naela heard the scrape of wood along stone as soon as she pushed open the door from the short, dark passageway. Mayfield came at her with a battered chair. She guessed he had been using it to wedge the handle in place. She ducked the chair and shoved the crazed doser to the floor with two fists to his back. She stomped on his kidneys to keep him down, though the action only heightened his wailing and shrieking.

Ben gave her quick work an approving nod before taking in the rest of their setting. Along one wall sparkled a pristine comm station standing like an altar under the pink flames of Hephestos's Breath.

101

"Jackpot," Ben said. "If there was an extant chip buried deep enough in this rock, it may have been protected from the flare and could still have communications capabilities." He sat down at the darkened controls.

"Don't." Mayfield's scream muffled into the stone floor. He said something else that Naela didn't catch so she pulled his head up enough to clear his speech.

"What was that?"

"Don't touch anything. Don't."

She let his head plop down with a small thud. When he tried to push himself up, she stepped harder on his lower back. "Any luck?"

"Not so far." Ben flicked a few switches and pushed some buttons, but the station remained inert. "Mayfield, you know if there is an extant emergency chip somewhere below?"

"No."

"No, there's no chip," Naela asked, "or, no, you don't know?"

"No," he said.

Ben walked all around the six by six meter station, which only took up half of the large empty room. His hands slid over every surface, including the roughhewn rock wall behind the comm setup. "Nothing."

Mayfield's body relaxed beneath Naela's weight.

"Wait. I have two manual levers over here."

Mayfield squirmed. "No."

"You must be on to something," Naela said.

"Now, which one to choose."

Mayfield pitched a fit and managed to wriggle out from under Naela's foot, all the while screaming, "Don't touch it. You'll kill us."

Before she could get another hand on him, Mayfield stabbed at her with a syringe he must have had secreted on his person. She twisted out of his reach, but his dosed-up body was fast. In an instant he was running at Ben, syringe held high above his head.

"It's taking too long. Too—"

Naela's knives in Mayfield's back cut him off and dropped him before Ben even spun around.

"I think we're evened up on the lifesaving," Ben said as he rolled Mayfield onto his side.

Blood dribbled from the man's mouth with each wet breath. Ben plucked the syringe from Mayfield's clenched fist. "What were you planning to stick me with? Some of that puma venom? Or another pharmacological goody?"

Mayfield stared intently into Ben's eyes, then let out a slow guttural laugh that rolled through the space like a cloud of sickness. Goosebumps rose on Naela's arms. It was as if that cloud pulled away the haze from the man's drug-addled mind. What was left reeked of calculation, malice, triumph.

"Now it's working." Mayfield whispered. "Now it's working." He coughed and wheezed, then clutched Ben's sleeve trying for one last gasp.

Naela stood over both men. Agitation put her on high alert. The harshness in her tone was meant for Mayfield, but with his death, she directed her anger at Ben. "What did he mean, 'now it's working'?"

Ben sat back on his heels in quiet consideration. "I guess his buzz kicked in," he finally said.

Naela would have felt more settled if a smile had accompanied the joke.

"Hmmm," was all she could reply.

"What are we sitting around for? We have a comm unit to fix." Ben went to the wall with the levers. "Which one?"

Naela saw she had stacked the knives on top of each other on Mayfield's right side. Since she was ambidextrous and didn't favor one hand over the other, she felt the alignment was as good of a sign as any. "Right."

The virtual painting above Javi's bed coalesced into pink and green swirls before a ribbon of blue bloomed in the center. Char had been here long enough to see this pattern repeat itself a dozen times.

"How's the big guy doing?"

She didn't even have to turn around at the voice—its tenor was a copy of Ben's, minus the heavy Yuraian accent. Because, unlike his younger brother, Colin Anlow was all polish and perfection, reminiscent more of a Socialite than an Armadan.

"Finally breathing on his own." She stroked Javi's cheek. "But he still hasn't regained consciousness yet."

Colin joined her at Javi's bedside. The barrister smelled like rain and maybe a hint of citrus. She wasn't used to an Armadan male indulging in scentbots so she always associated this smell exclusively with Colin.

"I think he just wanted an excuse for extra rack time."

"Rack time." Char actually smiled a little. "You sound more like a soldier every time I see you."

"Dreadfire sees me way too often in official capacities, if you ask me. I told Ben to invite all of you over to the lake house one of these years. I can handle a grill even better than a courtroom."

He'd certainly had to put his legal skills to work plenty of times for this team—and had never failed them. Ben was proud of his brother for that. The thought brought on a twinge of worry. "I need to tell you about Ben."

"Meke already filled me in."

"Any word?"

"Not yet. The auroras are making communications and retrieval impossible for now." He gave her a reassuring smile, much like Ben's, but she'd always thought Colin was…prettier, especially dressed in an expensive suit like this dark blue one with its side zip tunic. Still, not quite the looker their eldest brother, David, was, but neither of the older Anlows could compete with Ben's contagious air of happiness.

"We have our own problems right here," Colin said, his tone just shy of scolding.

"They started it," she said.

"No, you started it when you walked off that ship still carrying a weapon." Colin was all business now. "That's not like you."

"I had a lot on my mind." She angled her chin toward Javi.

"As did Aurelien, I surmise. I'm going to have to make a few deals to clean up this fiasco. Assaulting Embassy-sanctioned contractors Planetside, during an official event with Embassy staff present, *and* in full range of a dozen voyeurs? Deals, indeed."

Char shrugged. "At least it was only Harrigut Domes and not at the Hub."

"Don't underestimate these small territories. They have a propensity for melodrama, which will garner systemwide attention. A contractor/Armadan skirmish in their backyard while debuting their new ambasadora? This will play on their backplanet Media channels for years."

"Only years? Auri will be disappointed."

Lucky break.

A four centimeter square panel in the comm controls slid open, revealing a dark hole from which wafted cold air. A mechanical clacking sound became louder. Ben envisioned the lead box containing the extant chip rising on the simple mechanical pulley. It was protocol, at least in Planetside Armadan strongholds, to use rudimentary machines as a safeguard for high tech failure. It would seem the designers of this comm station studied at the same school of logic.

The leaden housing emerged from the hole enough that its bottom sat flush with the station desk. Ben picked up the heavy grey box and popped the lock.

"Does it look viable?" Naela asked.

"It's pretty enough to wear." He held the box for her to see as if presenting a gift.

Naela's smile suddenly fell into a wistful look of resignation. "Call your team, Lt. Anlow, but please don't tell them anything about me."

"Well, I think they're going to notice an extra passenger for pick up."

"I can't go with you." Her words were a sad whisper.

"What are you talking about? You can't stay here."

"Efrom saw me," she said. "The Embassy may already know of my disobedience. I can't go back to a writ on my head."

"I guess I hadn't taken that into consideration." A protective anger swept through him. After all this running, he wasn't abandoning her.

"Let me and my team take credit for the kill," he said. "All members of Dreadfire will give statements that you were never here, that in the confusion of battle, Contractor Efrom Starrie must have been mistaken. Don't take this the wrong way, but contractors look so much alike that it's not too farfetched."

"Probably the inbreeding."

"Your words, not mine," Ben was quick to point out, but he could see that she was simply adding some levity to the situation. He liked that about her.

"All of your team would swear to it?" she asked.

"Yes," he said without hesitation.

"Why?"

"Armadans are always looking for something to brag about," Ben lied.

"You trust your troopers that much?" she asked.

"They're like family," he said.

"That wouldn't mean much if you knew my family."

"There's no chance of convincing Efrom to give you a pass?" He thought of any number of his cousins and knew without a doubt they would do whatever it took to protect the family—no questions asked. Surely contractors weren't that different.

"Efrom will either bask in the glory of my capture, or worse, try to use it to force a final claim on me."

"Like marriage?"

"Which will allow him breeding rights. And, I will die before he touches me again."

"Again…" The word barely made it out of Ben's mouth because it carried implications he wasn't certain he wanted to hear.

"I was forced to make my first kill when I was twelve, but that trauma couldn't compare to the abuse Efrom and a few of my other cousins had been forcing upon me for the previous three years."

Her hand tapped against her thigh as she spoke, and he no longer saw it as an amusing superstition but for the mental coping mechanism that it was. He broke out in cold sweats trying not to picture Naela as a terrified little girl at the hands of her brutal cousins.

"I'm sorry. That's fucked up."

"No," she said, a hint of tears forming at the side of her ice blue eyes. "What's fucked up is that I thought it meant they cared about me. I was flattered by their attention at first until…"

"Didn't anyone put a stop to it in your family?" Ben asked.

"My half-brother, Nikos. He came home from training and an extended posting on Tampa Two. He beat Efrom senseless when he found out, and I idolized him for it. And, I wanted to show him how much in the only way I knew how." The tears flowed freely now.

Ben wanted to comfort her, but wasn't sure how she'd feel about being touched, so he stood there like a fool and just listened.

"He offered marriage that same year. I was a month shy of my sixteenth birthday. That night I made two life-changing decisions—I joined the Embassy's assassin program as a lifetime devotee under penalty of death, and I became celibate. Nikos was devastated, but he said his emotional fallacy for me wouldn't allow him to hate me."

She stared deep into Ben's eyes. "But *I* hated me, and so does Efrom. He's made it clear many times that in a society of multiple partners and selectively bred heightened hormones, I may as well be sterile.

"Only, a funny thing happened. My worth has actually increased over the past decade or so as word of my skills spread through the contractor community. Not only do I hail from one of the purest genetic families, but I am also an expert killer."

"Quite a legacy."

"Quite a horribly awful, pathetic legacy." Her shoulders hunched and she cried into her hands.

Witnessing the breaking of such a strong woman made Ben feel like an interloper. He shouldn't have been here to see this. But he *was* here, so he moved slowly and pulled her against him. She sobbed quietly and trembled while he sorted through his own emotions evoked by her lifetime of confessions. If it were him, he would have cried much sooner.

The block-sized chip skittered and clacked across the stone floor like an attacking insect.

"Useless," Ben said. Tossing the chip was the first sign of a temper Naela had seen from the easy-going man.

She picked the device up. "Why wouldn't they bury the extant circuitry farther down as well?"

"I guess they never expected the relay between the backup board and the station board to fry, too."

"What about your reporter?" she asked. "Can you power it with the chip?"

"Already tried. No juice." Ben put his head in his hand and leaned on the comm console. He let his eyelids fall and took a ragged breath.

He looked so tired. Dark circles pooled under his eyes. Maybe fatigue accounted for his edginess. Or low blood sugar. She walked over and put a hand on his shoulder. "Maybe we should have some lunch or dinner or maybe it's even breakfast…." There was no telling time now that Mayfield was dead and his body wrapped in large sheets of plastic from the kitchen.

"Or a nap," Ben said, patting her hand before he stood up. "But, first, I think we need to move our old friend to the greenhouse."

Naela carried Mayfield by his plastic-swaddled legs and Ben took his shoulders as they finagled the body back through the pantry, out of the living area, and stuck it in a corner of the greenhouse.

She could add another corpse to a long, informal list—three times as many as her official Embassy dossier counted at 278.

"Do you ever enjoy your kills?" she asked. "Or are you like me, often running from the violence in your life?"

"Lately…running has crossed my mind more than ever. Must be my age."

"You're thinking of leaving the Armada?"

"If I had reason to," he said.

"Isn't *wanting* to go reason enough?"

"Whatever would I do with myself?"

"No jokes," she said. "What would be enough to make you leave?"

Ben regarded her for a moment, his countenance turning serious. "A family."

She had expected to hear horrible things like death, pain, suffering. Even bureaucratic frustrations. But leave it to Ben Anlow to pull out a positive. With a surprising twinge of jealousy, she asked, "Are you not married yet?"

"Lots of Armadans marry late. Just kind of ends up that way."

"Because of tradition? Or is that part of what you're running from?"

Ben took on a joking tone, which Naela had learned was a concealment technique as much as her finger tapping. "Oh, someone thinks she knows all about me after these past few days together."

They sauntered back into the living quarters where Naela poured herself a glass of water and Ben helped himself to some more frost.

"I know that, like the Armadan stereotype, you enjoy a decent amount of alcohol."

He raised his glass to her before taking a sip.

She curled up on the couch and he joined her.

"What else do you know?" he asked.

"You probably come from a generational military family, which is quite wealthy, and your parents are a monogamous couple, a trait you plan to follow?"

"Well, first things first. *Most* Armadans are service-born, which is why they call it the Armada, or maybe why we're called Armadans. I don't really know. Anyway, and, yes, a lot of us have some blocks stashed for a rainy day or a system-wide uprising, whatever comes first."

She could actually imagine him surrounded by piles of blue currency blocks, building elaborate structures in a vault somewhere, then breaking them all apart for his own amusement or his children's.

"And your parents?" she asked. "Do they have any amours besides each other?"

"No," he said as if begrudging her the win. "It's just them. And, before you ask, yes, I would prefer to have only a prime, one woman to spend the rest of my long Armadan life with and raise a half-dozen babies."

"Interesting," she said, purposely veiling the excitement in her tone. The idea of having children had always felt like a curse to her. Ben's delight when he spoke of that kind of future had her second-guessing her perspective. Though she was careful to keep any daydreams in check.

"You think that sounds boring, don't you?" he asked.

It sounds perfect.

"My mother has eight amours," Naela said. "My father, who was her last amour and considerably younger, just married his sixth. And I find both of my parents extremely boring. I haven't spoken to either of them in over a decade."

"I guess that's one way to avoid the confusion of family dinners," Ben said hesitantly, as if testing her sense of humor about so touchy a subject.

"Especially when half of them are already related in one way or another."

Ben remained still, a small muscle in his cheek twitching.

She bumped her shoulder against his. "Don't tell me you didn't think that was funny."

He leaned in so close that she could feel his nose touch her ear and smell the clean scent of vodka on his breath. "I think you're very funny, Naela. And full of warmth and vulnerability and strength. And I feel like everything I went through since I met you was worth it just to discover the truth about Naela Starrie."

She kissed him. No hesitation, no guilt. Only passion and acceptance. And, perhaps the faintest of ideas in the back of her superstitious mind that coupling with Ben could balance the hurt from her past. Naela wouldn't let their lips part as she pulled him with her and lay back on the couch.

She lingered over every sensation, from running her fingers through his thick hair to rubbing her thumbs over the dark stubble framing his jaw. Though his hands were quite large, they were agile and precise in their movements over her body, even with the fabric of the pilfered clothing still covering her. His touch was surprisingly gentle and reassuring, allowing her to be the aggressor.

It may have been half a lifetime ago that she last docked, but her confidence never faltered. She kissed his neck, tasted the muskiness of his skin, and slid her hands under his shirt. His body was solid and his frame so much larger than a contractor's. When she was young, his type would have put her off. No grace in his form, no classic beauty in his features.

But as this Armadan officer oh-so-carefully stripped her of her clothes and stroked her and kissed her and pushed inside her, she could feel the grace flow from his hands, his mouth, and the pulsing of his hips. And when he smiled down at her and called her name in his rough accent, she knew she would never find a more beautiful human being here or on the Otherside. Ben Anlow was the dream she had stuffed down inside herself for too long.

I'm in trouble.

Ben grabbed a handful of dehydrated cherries from the bag on the counter and wandered into the comm station to find Naela examining the chip once again. He hadn't remembered falling asleep after their coupling or how long he'd been out. But forever imprinted in his mind was the feel and taste of her. He was definitely in over his head, maybe not quite *lost in her* as the derogatory expression went, but certainly losing ground to his feelings for her fast.

He wondered if her being gone when he woke up was a sign of some regret on her part or, worse, ambivalence. His concern irritated him. He truly wasn't himself. Maybe that's why he could justify his next statement, concealed as a joke, yet anything but. "I guess you're not the cuddling type."

As soon as she looked over at him and smiled, a wave of relief coursed through his chest. He felt ridiculous and was glad she couldn't see the emotional turmoil he hid inside.

She kissed his cheek in greeting and gave his forearm a friendly pulse. "You needed the rest, and though the couch is a delight to share for some things, sleeping isn't one of them. And, I wouldn't want to interrupt your afterglow."

He laughed. "If only we males could experience that kind of bliss just once."

"You can. In the V-side," she said.

"The virtual world? Thanks, but I'll pass."

"Have you never been to the V-side?" Naela asked.

"Not interested in the realm of fraggers." It was a decisive response.

"Afraid you'd have to give up some control?"

"Afraid I'd have to give up *all* control," Ben said.

"That's amusing coming from a gambler. I thought you found risk intoxicating."

"Risking money is different. Meaningless. I'm surprised you're a V-side advocate. You don't seem like the type to give up much control either....Oh, wait. You came *here* by yourself."

"Hmm," she said.

"By the way, how long was I out?"

"A few hours."

"Hours?" Apparently the strain of this adventure was manifesting in fatigue. He pushed out the warning claxon in the back of his mind that reminded him that he could easily stay up for five days straight, *without* the help of stims, and still function at ninety percent.

"Do you feel okay?" Naela asked, as if reading his mind.

He wanted to be off the subject immediately. "Yeah. You have a breakthrough with that chip?"

"No, but I think I know what this is for." She double-tapped a finger to the left lever on the wall. "See that partition over there?"

"The metal section…" Even as he was saying it he realized how obvious it was now. "It's a shield. Probably a window underneath there."

"My thoughts, too. Perhaps that's what Mayfield didn't want you to open."

"Maybe. But this could be our backdoor out of here, assuming Efrom's gang is coming in the same way we did."

"A possible escape plan, but we're hardly outfitted for the temperatures and weather at this elevation."

"We may not have a choice." Ben didn't like their options much either.

"Your team could get here first," Naela said.

Time to consider the reality. "Chances are they won't make it before the Embassy sends in another group. One of our troopers was attacked in the cave on our journey here."

"The puma you asked Mayfield about."

"A fucking venomous puma, if you can believe that shit." Ben's voice trailed off a bit in thought as he said, "Probably the same stuff Mayfield tried to give us."

"Do you think it's safe?"

"The needle never punctured my skin…." Ben zoned out for a moment.

"No, I mean is it safe to raise the shield?"

"Oh. Sure. I can't imagine Stavros, or the Embassy, or whoever really owns this place, would leave a faulty window and shield to chance at this elevation." Ben gripped the emergency release handle with both hands. "You may want to wait in the living quarters, though. Just in case."

She stepped up right next to him. "I'd rather fly out of that window with you than stay here and wait for Efrom on my own."

Ben had to put more effort into lifting this lever. He hoped it was because this one was simply stuck and not that his strength was waning so badly. Once the lever clicked into place, the shield rolled up into the ceiling on its own.

No freezing cyclone of wind lashed out to pull them through the opening— only a blinding wave of green and pink light. Once Ben's eyes adjusted to the increased brightness, he was rendered speechless. The night landscape swayed before him as a shimmering aurora undulated across the sky and among the peaks of Chumbal Range where it met an electrifying albedo of the same fluorescent color scheme.

Naela's hand curling around his anchored him to this unique setting. He knew he'd never experience so overwhelming a moment like this again, no matter if he lived the rest of his one hundred odd years in full. The emotion radiated through his chest and where his hand nestled around Naela's. Neither of them spoke. They never even looked at each other. They simply basked in the scene… and in each other's comforting presence.

That little fucking bastard.

Ben popped another handful of dried fruit into his mouth. He'd been feeling the shakes, like when his blood sugar was low, but he knew it was something more. His symptoms were the same as Javi's but on a smaller, slower scale.

Naela watched the aurora and he watched her. He would admit to his own prejudices about contractors, yet he found Naela's culture fascinating.

"Are you watching me, Lt. Anlow?"

"About as intently as you're watching the auroras."

"It puts me at peace. The combination of pink and green with an occasional indigo is like a giant synth spider weaving the light above the planet instead of over Carrey Bay," she said. "Only, no music to guide the patterns."

"I could always sing for you."

"I don't think you feel like singing." She placed a cool hand on his fevered cheek and studied his eyes. "It was the frost, wasn't it? Mayfield dosed it with some of that venom. That was his plan to handle Efrom or anyone else he deemed a threat."

"Yeah, I don't believe it was a coincidence that those bottles were the only ones sitting out."

"I'm glad I killed that coward."

Ben cupped his hand over hers. "Me, too. And, I guess now we know what the little fucker's last words meant. He could see in my eyes that the poison had finally started to take root. Apparently I wasn't drinking fast enough. Or maybe my tolerance was just higher than expected."

She pulled away and bolted for the kitchen like an alarm had gone off. "There has to be an antidote." She pulled open drawers and slammed them back shut. "He would have made one, right? And, why didn't I get sick?" A row of cabinets felt her wrath next.

He was touched at her concern. "You had one sip before you threw your mug at Mayfield. And, I've looked this place over a hundred times already."

Probably one hundred and two.

"I found a few vials with clear fluid, but they're unmarked," he continued. "I'm a gambler, but if that's more venom and not a cure…well, let's just say I lose to the house ninety-eight percent of the time."

She tossed the mostly empty bottle of alcohol against the stone wall. Glass sprayed in a rainbow of color over every surface of the grey and white kitchen and all over Naela. She grabbed another one, this one full, and threw it. Then another and another. Screaming in between.

Before she could go for the mugs next, Ben hugged her from behind. "It's slow-acting. I'm still standing and still thinking. But I need you to be the woman who single-handedly beheaded one of the worst serial murderers this system has ever seen. I need that, Naela. Okay?" His words were laced with patience and confidence because that's how he felt. He was definitely a calm-before-the-storm type of guy.

Even if this storm is my last.

"Then we need to make preparations in case Efrom gets here before your team returns," she said, pushing away from him, but unable to look him in the eyes.

"And, if the Embassy's rescue team gets here before both of them and finds you?"

"Let me worry about that. I know their protocol best."

"Okay," he was reluctant to let the possibility go, but knew they could only concentrate on the more immediate threat. "Ready to go guerilla on your fucking cousin?"

On the edge of wakefulness, Naela listened to see whether the tapping she'd heard would stay in her dreams or carry over to the real world. Only Ben's light snoring sounded within the bedroom.

A chill crept along her leg and hand. She pulled them back under the blankets and snuggled her body against Ben. His arm slid around her waist and warm breath exhaled against the nape of her neck. She splendored in the lethargy of half-sleep. It had been more mornings than she cared to count since she'd woken up in a man's arms. Or since she feared losing someone.

Their time here at Durstal Ki was a fantasy. This moment epitomized the past few days—surreal and isolated. She enjoyed the dreamy blissful nature of both as much as the safe harbor of Ben's embrace.

She had forgotten about the outside world, but knew it would rush back upon them with a vengeance. If neither of them died on this mountain, they'd still never see one another again. She'd lied when she said she'd come up with a contingency for evading the Embassy. Even if Ben's team did get her out first, Sovereign Simon Prollixer had a long reach—she'd be lucky if she could hide out for the rest of her life in a mud hut in Archenzon.

Maybe death was preferable. At least on the Otherside, Naela believed that she and Ben would have a chance to start again.

"I can hear you thinking." He spoke softly into her hair—his voice rough with sleep and his Yurain brogue extra strong with the rolling *R* and elongated vowels.

She ran her fingers through the hair on his arm in response, not wanting to speak and ruin the magic of the morning. If she didn't acknowledge him, she could pretend all was well, that he wasn't dying slowly and….

"Is it painful? The venom?" she asked.

"Not so much."

He was lying. She noticed him hanging his head last night and squinting his eyes. His breathing sounded labored now, not simply from sleep.

"Let me bring you some water. Some food." She tried to get up, but his arm held her fast.

"Maybe just stay here a little longer. It's a good moment."

Alarm tingled through her at the finality in his voice. He'd never spoken of defeat the entire time they had been together. Her anger rose.

And, you're not giving up now.

"No." She pushed away from him and stood. Though her voice quavered, she barked orders at him. "You're getting up. You're going to eat something and you're going to help me finish our preparations."

He smiled one of his lazy smiles that she'd grown so fond of and gave her a mock salute. "Yes, sir."

Then he became fully alert and sat up, listening. She heard it, too. A scraping noise, similar to the tapping of her dreams, traveled from the greenhouse into the living quarters and shattered their private sanctuary.

"They're here," she said.

The rustic alarms sounded as dozens of metal forks and spoons jingled against stone. The real world was coming for them. Denial had kept her deaf and blind until it was almost too late.

They grabbed their weapons and took positions on either side of the door. Ben motioned for Naela to move ahead and scout while he covered her with his rifle. With twenty projectile rounds left, they'd need to be smart.

She kept her knives sheathed to avoid reflecting the scant light of Hephestos's Breath, but her fingers gripped the metal handles in preparation for combat.

She raised two fingers and pointed to her right side, then pointed over her shoulder to the left—an Armadan signal Ben had taught her earlier to relay numbers and location. Then she flashed three fingers twice and made a circular motion to indicate six more running the perimeter.

Ben crept closer. Sweat dripped from his brow, but his jaw showed a tense focus. He moved the index finger lying alongside the trigger just enough to give her the go-ahead for the first part of their plan. Like the alarm, their defenses were of primitive design, but effective warfare wasn't created in this millennia. Efrom was about to find out that it's not about the advanced nature of the technology, it's about the cleverness of the users.

The footsteps slapped rapidly against the stone now that the silverware traps had exposed the contractors' positions. They closed in from multiple sides.

Naela grabbed the end of Ben's surplus steel nylon rope which they had substituted for the chains on one side of the hanging flower beds along this sector. A single yank undid the system of special knots and sent the closest sides of six massive gardens plummeting to the floor with an ear-splitting crash. The other sides hung tight by their original chains and formed a wall of metal between the intruders and their quarry.

Startled shouts and weapons fire filled the warehouse-size space. Water from the hydroponic units puddled around heaps of ejected foliage and squirming bioluminescent proto-shrimp.

Though none of the contractors had sustained injuries, Ben and Naela knew what they needed so as not to fight blindly—Efrom's group had projectile weaponry and they were now corralled outside of a zone that surrounded the living quarters.

A female contractor closest to them popped around the bed barrier and fired. The bullet made dust of the stone a meter above Naela's head. She ducked down and went for the second rope.

A single report from Ben's rifle answered back. "Got her."

"Ready for phase two," Naela said.

With a hard pull, she tore away a piece of the overhead utility track they had weakened earlier. One of the mechanical tending machines stuffed with a dozen full bottles of vodka plummeted to the floor just in front of the barrier. She heaved on a third rope. Flares, their triggers knotted within the steel nylon, shot down at the spreading alcohol and liquid batteries to ignite in a series of blinding red fireballs.

Naela caught sight of flames ripping up both sides of another contractor before she had to shield her eyes. His screams told her that he'd be out of commission, if the blaze didn't kill him outright.

Gunfire eclipsed the burning man's shrieks. Muzzle flashes lit up the darker corners away from the inferno. The heat sent Ben and Naela scurrying back into the living quarters.

"Time for phase four," Ben said.

"Three," Naela corrected.

"Yeah, three." Ben looked around as though puzzling out where he was.

Naela hadn't missed the slur in his speech either. A sure sign the venom was finally compromising him.

"Ben, are you with me?"

He downed a bottle of water and tossed it to the cut stone floor. "Yep. But I am fading. We have to get rid of them soon."

Even with the highly flammable liquid batteries in the alcohol mix, the fire would burn out within the next half hour.

"They've stopped firing," Ben said. "That means they're on the move."

"Then it's time for the next phase. Do you see any of them yet?"

Ben kneeled behind a counter and rested his rifle against the top. No doubt he needed the surface to steady the scope. His arms twitched constantly now.

"Two on the move to the left. Trying to find a weak spot in the barrier. I don't see the rest, but I'm betting they kept a spotter in place back in that dark corner and sent the remaining four to come in from the right."

Smart.

It was the weakest part of the barricade plan. The farthest bed would still leave a space at bottom big enough for a small person to shimmy through once the flames died down enough.

Naela scurried to the other side of the doorway. From here she could see directly into the weak spot. She grasped a sharpened butter knife from the collection of repurposed cutlery laid out carefully along the wall beside her. Her throwing skills were the first defense so they could conserve their precious bullets until the end.

Ben's rifle staccatoed with four shots.

"Fuck. My reflexes are going. Can't keep an easy pressure on the trigger. Didn't even wound one of those assholes."

"You pushed them back. They'll think twice before trying another assault from that direction."

Without acknowledging her patronizing words, he brought the scope back up and breathed in a long, ragged breath.

A shadow near the barricade crawlspace pulled Naela's attention. She forced herself to breathe normally. At the first sign of the shadow returning, she exhaled and targeted it with the butter knife. The shadow fell away from the breech. She readied a blade in each hand. A metal glint flashed by her and sliced through the long-sleeved shirt and her bicep.

Razor disc.

Judging the angle of her attacker, she released both knives in that direction before crouching down.

Ben shot again, but this time he managed only two rounds and a quiet, "Got that bastard."

Gunfire crackled all around them, coming from both sides. Naela scrambled on her knees away from the doorway to avoid the crossfire.

Ben, safe behind the counter, fired to the left again three times.

The onslaught continued. By now, Efrom would have realized they were rationing their ammo. And the fires died down to knee height. Shadows entered the breech. Naela hurled a quick succession of a half a dozen knives at the contractors, then yelled, "Incoming," as she ran for the counter.

"Clear the breech." Efrom pushed the wounded contractor ahead of him through the opening.

Naela's ingenuity exhilarated him. She did her line proud with both her intelligence and courage. She'd bear him magnificent children.

A knife glanced off the metal bed a few centimeters from his ear.

He just had to convince her how satisfying that match would be. He planned to take his time and enjoy the convincing.

With one last contorted turn of his shoulder, he popped through the barricade. He plastered himself against the wall. The Armadan with Naela might be running low on ammunition or it could have been a ruse to make the contractors let down their guard. Efrom knew better than to take chances with a fleet officer's aim. Between that man and Naela, they had managed to take out all but four of Efrom's team.

Tokaki crawled through the breeched opening and joined him at the wall. He could barely see Carson along the other end of the barrier. He was apparently the only one left on that side. Efrom dropped a hand signal once Pablo scrambled up beside Tokaki. Carson made a move to climb the barrier.

Two shots fired from inside the living quarters, but the aim was wide. Carson kept tracking forward, firing his own weapons, a pair of projectile handguns that still had the familiar heft of cenders.

Efrom slipped around the doorframe in a crouch and opened fire in the direction he estimated the Armadan to be. Tokaki passed behind Efrom with Pablo on her tail. No one was in sight. The contractors took cover behind various furnishings in the living room. Efrom didn't have a clear vantage of the kitchen from his position, but he could hear a subtle scraping noise coming from that general direction.

Carson crept through the doorway to their rear. Another step and a silver handle thudded into his chest, then a second into his neck.

Efrom risked standing to see Naela dragging the Armadan from the kitchen into a pantry.

"We have them."

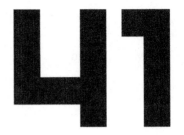

Popping from overheated circuitry joined the occasional weapons fire as Naela maneuvered Ben through the secret hallway.

She laid his head on the stone floor of the comm station as gently as she could in her haste, then raced back into the passageway, intent on the last phase of their plan. Actually, this was the alternative to phase four—the failsafe they hoped they wouldn't have to use because there wasn't much chance of surviving it.

By the time she reached the pantry door, Efrom was standing there. He held double handguns on her.

"It's over, Naela." He lowered his pistols ever so slightly. "I can help you with this—"

She dove for the side and came rolling back up with a weapon in hand. She swung the homemade club made from a wooden chair leg imbedded with sharpened spoons.

Efrom leapt out of the way. Naela's weapon crashed into the male contractor just behind him with a dull thud.

She scanned the floor.

Where?

She spotted the end of the last piece of Ben's grappler rope between the feet of the female contractor. Before the woman had a chance to fire in the crowded space of the pantry, Naela rushed her. Their bodies traveled together with Naela's shoulder in the woman's abdomen until a shelf arrested their momentum.

Naela pushed off the stunned contractor and zeroed in on the rope's end. Her fingers brushed it, but Efrom brought his gun down across the side of her head. She fell forward. Thankful that he hadn't landed a direct blow to her temple, Naela kicked out and caught his right knee. The knock-back sent him reeling enough for her to scrabble toward the pantry door again.

She went for the rope end on a second try. This time she snatched it just as Efrom grabbed her by the leg and tossed her to the side.

Too late.

His action had pulled the rope and brought the bulky metal pantry shelves crashing down against the walls. As hundreds of kilograms of food stuff rained from above, Naela rolled into the secret hallway. Before Efrom could lay another hand on her, she slammed the small door shut.

She dragged over the huge five kilo buckets of lipids they'd put in here earlier and blocked the entry completely. Then just before she slammed the door leading into the comm station, she kicked away the release for the cart they'd wheeled in. Off-balance, it tipped toward the closing door. Its cargo, a broken-down mechanical gardener thudded against the metal, effectively sealing Ben and her into the comm station.

Naela?

The squeal of crashing metal brought a bit of consciousness back to Ben. His returning vision registered a wall of white. It was painfully bright, yet he refused to close his eyes against it because already darkness crept along the edges. He was afraid he wouldn't wake up next time.

A cough rattled in his chest and dispelled the encroaching unconsciousness. He felt a cold hand on his cheek, then a form blocked some of the light...Naela standing in front of the window.

She stooped down next to where he was propped against the back of the comm desk.

"Glad you're back with me," she said.

"I guess I missed phase four." Speaking agitated the wet cough and sent him into a fit of spasms that blazed inside his chest like he'd inhaled fire.

"We never made it to phase four," Naela said.

He took shallow breaths and whispered, "Sorry I wasn't much help. I don't remember—" Coughing took him despite his most careful efforts.

Naela sat down beside him and held his shoulders as he fought to breathe.

"It happened fast," she said. "Too fast. A group stormed the barricade on one side while Efrom and the others snuck through the breech. You took out one of them before you went down."

She cradled his head on her shoulder. "I thought you'd been shot." She cleared her throat. "There were so many bullets flying around back there."

"How many of those fuckers are left?"

"By my count, only Efrom and a female."

"Then you have a chance," Ben said.

"*We* have a chance." She pulled away to face him. "Ben, *we* have a chance."

He tried a smile and repeated, "*We* have a chance." Here was his opening. "But only if you blow the frame on that window and get the hell out of here."

"To get help, you mean?" Her tone and expression said she saw through his ruse. "It will take two injured contractors a very long time to reach us in here. And, we cached enough supplies for at least a week."

Ben shook his head. She stilled it with a finger under his chin. "Your team will be back for you by then."

He captured her fingers and said, "Promise me, Naela. If your cousin or his friend get through that door, you'll pop that window frame like we have it rigged and get out of here."

"I promise."

He saw in her eyes how easy it was for contractors to lie.

Naela panicked in the silence. Ben's coughing had stopped, and she took that as a very bad sign because she could barely hear him breathing now.

"Ben. Ben." Naela gently slapped his cheek, then walloped him good when there was no response.

A tiny groan was the only response.

"Open your eyes. Ben." She tugged one lid up, but there wasn't a pupil response. *He won't last the night.*

Denial and rage gripped her at the realization. She pushed up from the makeshift bed she'd assembled for him on the hard stone and stood at the window. Beyond was a spectacle so gripping she wanted to weep. Flowing waves of chartreuse and magenta chased sharp striations of lavender and tangerine behind the Chumbal Range as sunset gave way to aurora. The radiation was fading, though—its brilliance now dulled in the inky murk of night.

She scratched at her wrist, forgetting the cut from her earlier skirmish with Efrom. Their tussle had somehow shifted her imbedded reporter so that a small corner jabbed at the skin underneath when she moved it in a certain way.

An idea whispered to her in desperate tones. If her implant circuitry was still viable, she could reboot it with the energy chip. The thermabots had lasted past the first of the flare....

She picked up the chip between thumb and forefinger and asked the Cosmos to repay her the luck it had stolen from her as an abused child, as a disenfranchised teenager, and as a lonely adult. She placed the chip in Ben's hand because she would need his luck, too.

Then, reciting chants in a tongue long dead, taught to her by a crazy old woman in the Palomin Desert, Naela picked up her knife and sliced her wrist.

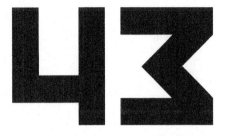

"Naela."

Efrom woke to ringing in his ears and pain in his chest. He pulled shallow breaths and focused his eyes. Stone and metal and…chai. He'd dreamt he was sitting in a hotel lobby with Naela drinking a cup of the sweet liquid, but the aroma surrounded him even upon waking. Balls of tightly wrapped tea leaves the size of his wrist communicator nodule decorated the floor around him. In fact, they rested against his face.

Understanding dawned upon him as he got his bearings. He was laid out on the pantry floor. Panic set in as he realized one of the metal shelves and the bulk of its contents pinned him to the stone. Efrom contorted his body and twisted his arm at a painful angle, then used the adrenaline provided by his fear to heave the shelf just enough to the side that he could crawl free.

There wasn't room to stand without one foot on a half-collapsed box of sugar packets and the other astride a metal crossbrace from a shelving unit.

"Tokaki."

A groan from his left. Somewhere.

"Can you talk, Tokaki?"

"Here." The word was raspy and faint, but allowed Efrom to zero in on her location.

He caught sight of her black sleeve against the beige boxes and tubs. He threw aside a dented container whose label had ripped off. Heavy liquid sloshed inside. He exposed Tokaki's blood-stained face. A torso-sized plastic barrel of wheat flour still lay atop the shelf crumpled around her legs and abdomen. He gave the grain a push with his shoulder and sent it rolling a half meter over the other side of the shelf.

"Can you stand?" he asked.

Tokaki was slow to respond. Efrom didn't have time for dallying. He grabbed her by the forearm and tugged her to a sitting position.

She cried out and slapped his hand away. "I can get up myself," she mumbled.

Her first attempt exposed a sprained, or perhaps broken, ankle. She fell back to the pile of debris. Not waiting for her to recover, Efrom pulled her upright once again. He did at least let her find her balance on her good leg. After all, his odds would be better with a backup, even an injured one.

"Grab the other end of that shelving unit," he said.

"We don't have the space to remove all this debris from the door." Her tight tone spoke of pain and resentment.

"We don't have to remove it all. Just enough for me to use this." He held up a grey square the size of his thumbnail.

"Explosive." Tokaki's expression showed incredulity. "That was on you? How did you not blow yourself up during the battle?"

"Latest experimental tech from our Embassy scientists. The explosive remains inert until I mix it with the primer." He opened his palm to reveal a second square of the same size, only bright red.

"Impressive." Despite her present condition, Efrom could tell by the new lilt of Tokaki's voice that he had won back her admiration. She most likely was imagining the fanfare they would receive for bringing down one of the system's most notorious "rogue" assassins. He and Tokaki would have their pick of assignments and posts.

But first they needed to knock on Naela's door.

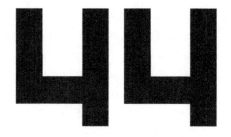

Naela slammed drawers and toppled sundry items from the comm desk. She gave up and scanned the comm room once more for one of Mayfield's drug stashes. Normally, she could deal with pain, but her implanted reporter was connected directly to the nerve cluster in her wrist. She could really use a stim to help her focus. Exposing the reporter's circuitry and attaching the energy chip was taking its toll on her mental fortitude.

Fourth time.

She sat back down on the floor and wiped sweat from her brow and blood from the metallic bulb which served as the communication device's brain.

Taking a breath then exhaling slowly, she pinched the tiny wire she'd pried from the circuitry with her fingernails. Too bad Mayfield hadn't squirreled away tweezers or a set of pliers in here. She may have been able to rewire the reporter to the chip the first time around with some tools.

She shoved the *what ifs* out of her mind. This was what she had to work with. She glanced over at Ben. This was what she had to do.

Bending the millimeter length of the stiff wire upright once again, she lined it up with a power node on the chip—now only the size of her thumbnail without its protective casing.

She involuntarily tensed her muscles, as she had each time, preparing for the inevitable zap from her nervous system. After all, she was the battery in this connection.

Node aligned with the wire, she eased the tiny opening toward the tiny lead.

Thank the Cosmos my natural eyesight is still so good.

Without the aid of her illegal tech this procedure was certainly more difficult. She exhaled one more time…

The concussive blast from somewhere inside the greenhouse or living area caused Naela to jerk her hand away, ruining the attempt to connect.

She placed the chip carefully on the comm desk, then ran for the blockaded door. Seconds passed. Minutes passed. No sounds from beyond, even when she held her ear up to the metal bed frame she'd stood on end and braced over the doorway. It was a good conductor of sound, but right now it offered only silence.

There were two possibilities: Efrom had been a victim of the explosion or he had caused it.

Though she wasn't sure how he'd accomplished it, she believed the blast was of Efrom's making. He was coming for her. She ran a hand along the metal bed frame. She indulged little confidence that it or the mechanical gardener would hold up to a second explosion.

That Efrom had not given up his hunt chilled her. Deep down she understood that way one or another, this was going to end badly.

But she was never one to miss the ending.

She resumed her spot on the stone floor beside Ben. Ignoring the tear-stirring pain, she straightened the wire from her reporter again. Maybe the pressure of knowing Efrom was on his way would help. Maybe she'd zap her system and stop her heart. Maybe the message would never make it to Ben's team. Maybe—

She reminded herself that *maybes* were just as bad as *what ifs* and lined up the chip's node.

Char took a glossy black box from the top of Matt's stack. The tantalizing smell of roasted duck, warm edamame salad, and buttered chrysanthemum flowers wafted on the steam escaping from under the lid. She put the meal on Javi's tray, but he'd dozed off again.

The mood of the group had brightened dramatically in this sterile room since Javi had regained consciousness. He was still weak, but Char had seen him rally some impossible strength when he was at his worst.

Matt handed her another box and passed out the rest.

"I'm starved," Auri said. "Even after eating the watery soup and stale crackers they left for me in the detention center."

"You were only detained for a day," Matt said.

"Confinement brings on my appetite."

"Everything brings on your appetite," Char said. It was good to have the team back together again.

Well, most of the team.

She glanced at Colin, the only one enjoying his boxed meal in somehow elegant style.

"He looks lonely, doesn't he?" Meke watched him too—hadn't been able to take her eyes off him since she got here, in fact. Maybe a man like him would tame a bit of her wild side.

"I think he needs a dinner date," Char urged.

"Colin Anlow probably has more dinner dates than he could attend in a lifetime," Meke said.

Char conceded the truth of that statement. The rest of the team had odds on Meke becoming the barrister's fifth amour, but Char knew better. Meke didn't like competing when the odds were against her.

Granted, Colin Anlow definitely preferred Armadan women, but not one of his other amours had served in the military. Char believed it was because he harbored guilt about not enlisting himself. His father and eldest brother, David, had certainly disapproved of Colin's occupational choice, but Ben had been supportive.

Ben was supportive of them all.

"What harm is there in flirting?" Char asked. Good nature washed over and through her now that Javi was recovering.

"You always make such compelling arguments," Meke told Char, then shifted her attention. "Colin." She pushed a long lock of honey red hair behind her ear. "I love hearing you talk. Your speech is always so eloquent."

Matt dropped his fork and spattered potato salad onto Char's boot.

"Way to go, idiot." Char wiped the mess off with her napkin.

Matt just mumbled.

"Hazard of the job," Colin said with a wink. "And my mother wouldn't have it any other way."

"Then why does Ben always sound decidedly *less than eloquent*?" Char asked.

"Most likely it's his ill-placed expletives."

"Ben's fucking expletives are just fine," Matt said around a mouthful of chicken.

"Nobody's fucking asking," Javi said from his bed.

Whoops of delight at hearing Javi's voice sounded from all around.

"Look who woke up in time for dinner." Char smoothed down one of his eyebrows. "Want to sit up?"

"I can do it." His tone wasn't mean, just forceful. A good sign.

"You can have my green stuff," Matt said.

"Are you already finish—"

Auri stood up suddenly, spilling his empty box and silverware to the tile floor and interrupting Char.

"Turn your reporters on," the trooper said.

"You can't have that on in a medical zone," Colin said.

But Char had hers up and running again instantly.

"It's a message. About Ben." She looked at Colin. "And, it's not good."

Bang, bang, bang.

Rattles, thuds, and scrapes resounded against the door to the secret hallway, followed by muffled yelling.

As Naela suspected, Efrom and the female had used the explosion to clear a path from the pantry.

It had taken them only an hour, exactly the amount of time Naela had sat here on this hard stone floor, careful not to disturb her transmitting reporter. The set up was precarious at best, using the coordinates Ben had already plugged into the comm station. Any slight movement could have joggled the wire out of the node. But she made sure not to move, aching muscles and sleeping limbs be damned.

LT. COMMANDER BEN ANLOW NEEDS ARMED PICK UP. TAMPA 3 COORDINATES—4.30 / 6.24 / 6.13.

There would be no reply, at least not one that Naela could receive, as she hadn't been able to recover all functions of her reporter. If Dreadfire hadn't heard her call for help yet, it would already be too late anyway.

She disconnected the chip, tied a piece of her shirt—well, Mayfield's shirt— around her bleeding wrist and put one final plan into action.

The constant efforts to gain entry pounded in her head like a meditation. Rather than the anticipatory fear she'd nursed since the explosion, she now filled her body with calm focus through every breath. That old woman at Palomin would be shocked that Naela could finally find her center while preparing to fight for her life.

She entered the blind she had fashioned around Ben. Metal cabinet doors they'd taken from the kitchen and stashed here earlier served as fort walls adjoining the space between the back of the comm desk and the window. The bright rays of light spread into obtuse angles as the sun fell far from its zenith. She was counting on Efrom's bad timing to play this natural defense against him.

Before anything else, Naela crouched down to check on Ben. His labored breathing said he was still alive. The flutter in his eyelids when she touched his shoulder said there was still hope.

"Ben, can you hear me?"

One of his hands twitched in acknowledgment. She grabbed it and squeezed. "Things are about to become noisy and probably a little bloody, but you need to hold on because I sent a message to Dreadfire. Just hold on until they get here."

He gave a small pulse to her hand and muttered something.

She put her ear close to his mouth.

"Stim."

Her heart fell. The pain must have been unbearable for him to ask for relief.

"I wish I had one to give you."

"Vest."

She scanned his body armor for a pocket or concealed pouch. A small zipper tab stuck out from a side seam on his right. Inside were a handful of stim patches he must have lifted from Mayfield's private dispensary.

"Is it safe? What if…nevermind." She had given up on *what ifs*.

She peeled the protective backing away from the stim and pressed its tiny tri-needles into his carotid artery.

Ben gasped. His chest rose from the floor, then fell back. He drew a huge breath, sat up, and pulled her into a kiss.

Before she realized what he was doing, he injected himself with a second stim. His pupils doubled in size and his hands shook.

"We finish this together." His voice was so weak, his words so slurred, that she barely recognized the accent she had grown such affection for.

She smoothed the pained wrinkles on his forehead and pushed away the sweat with her thumb. "Together."

The ruckus at the door suddenly ceased.

"Stay down." Naela huddled into Ben, their heads covered with their arms.

A boom echoed through the stone walls of the comm room, then Naela heard nothing but high-pitched ringing as debris smashed into the desk, cracked the window, and rained down upon Ben and her.

Before the dust even cleared, she had her last few knives at the ready. A signal from Ben, then he popped up over the desk and fired his rifle while Naela vaulted over the side of the blind and ran for Efrom.

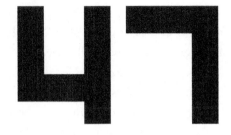

The ringing in Naela's ears made the world seem to slow down.

When Ben opened fire, Efrom spun away from the blasted entry and back into the hallway. The female made it into the comm room, then somersaulted to the right and managed cover within an alcove where the pink flames served as a natural sconce.

The direct angle of a close sun opaqued the dust clouds inside with ultra-bright rays of light. Essentially blind and deaf, Naela hunted on instinct. After decades of fear inspired by her cousin, she would now make him the prey. And she had learned quite a bit since she was a little girl.

Another shot from Ben's rifle sounded like a *whiff* through Naela's tinnitus. Answering *whiffs* came from the decorative alcove.

With the female's attention on Ben, Naela scurried to the wall housing the half-blown entry. Making herself as flat as possible, knives in a fighting position, she waited.

The muzzles of Efrom's guns appeared first.

She waited.

Slowly they penetrated the swirling glare of dust, exposing his finger on the trigger a mere half a meter from her shoulder.

She waited.

Gripped hands gave way to long black sleeves covering wrists.

She struck.

Efrom's gun fell from his grip as Naela sliced through the tendons of his closest wrist. Blood spurted high. In a flash she spun into the entryway and plunged the other knife toward Efrom's chest.

But her shoulder kinked with pain and she couldn't follow through with the stab.

The *whiffs* became louder, fighting the ringing in her ears.

Naela had a split second to realize the female had tagged her with a shot to the arm before Efrom was upon her.

Shit.

Ben spotted the blood on Naela's shoulder and hoped it was only a flesh wound. He was fading and he was failing. Rage welled up inside him, adding to the stim effects. He welcomed the red haloing his vision.

Blood lust. A mythical Armadan trait that had more of a basis in reality than anyone would ever let on. He used it with the last of his strength, acting as if in a dream.

Vaulting over the desk, he rushed the alcove, swimming through dust motes in a sea of light. The range too close for accuracy, he flipped his battle rifle around to access the bludgeoning end.

The contractor kept her aim on Naela. Shock registered in her expression just before Ben brought the butt of his gun down on her temple. She crumpled.

But so did he. Down on his knees. The impact not registering in his pain center, in his brain. He put out a hand to catch himself and sent the rifle clattering away on the stone.

Naela.

He wanted to see her one last time before the end.

But the darkness took him first.

The ringing subsided enough for Naela to hear Efrom's voice in muffled rage. It spurred memories of humiliation and abuse within her. She welcomed the emotions.

Light strobed into shadow within the confines of the comm room and played over the battle for Efrom's weapon like a trite metaphor. Naela had hold of his wrist so the remaining gun pointed at the carved-out ceiling. She was not a match for his physical strength, but she had tricks.

Always have tricks.

Using the wall for leverage, she flipped over his shoulder and stripped him of the weapon.

From this new direction she caught a glimpse of the strobe's source. A heliocraft's blades spun outside the window. Another craft closed in fast behind it.

It would seem both friend and foe had joined the fray.

Naela evaded a kick to her abdomen from Efrom, but had to absorb a strike to her neck from the edge of his hand. Her limbs worked in practiced motion— blocking, parrying with her knife, landing her share of blows.

But Efrom was practiced too, and in the same fighting style. It was a familial dance, wrought with old hatreds and hierarchies.

And Efrom was about to be dethroned.

She feinted a parry, knew he would go for the punch to her kidney, and was ready to slice his neck when a rapid succession of *thunks* peppered the window outside.

Naela sprang out of the way when she saw a trooper swinging from the heliocraft, headed for the window feet first, energy blasts lighting up the end of her battle rifle.

Char shot repeatedly into the portion of glass that was already spiderwebbed and hoped it was damaged enough to crumple under her accelerating mass.

Matt and Auri were barreling down the grappler line directly behind her. They'd all go crunch if that reinforced glass didn't give.

She breathed and relaxed her body for impact. A broken ankle—or neck—wouldn't do Ben any good.

Concussive waves rippled through her joints and muscles as her boots made contact with the window. But it gave way and shattered. She cut her connection to the line and tucked into a roll. She was on her feet after one rotation and training her rifle on the two contractors inside.

Through her weather mask she asked, "Ben Anlow. Where is he?"

Matt and Auri popped up next to her.

Meke's voice broke into the co-com. *You were right, Char. This new ship is Embassy. Filled with contractors. Must have seen us and changed course from their original bearing on the fortress.*

"Make sure they know this is an official Armadan rescue operation," Char said.

"You have no authority here," the male contractor facing her here inside said.

"I have a man down. That and this battle rifle give me all the authority I need." She tapped her visor to retract it from her face.

The chill of buffeted winds nearly stole her breath, but she could see much better. In fact…. "Stop. Don't go near him." She tracked the female contractor crawling on the floor toward Ben's still form.

"Auri, check him out." Char tensed. So, help her, if Ben was dead, she'd take both of these fucking contractors out and call it self-defense.

As if in response to her thoughts, a voyeur zipped in through the broken window. One of theirs. At first she cursed Meke for sending in the ball of cameras and microphones, but knew having eyes and ears on them would force everyone to be on their best behavior.

And the attendees to this soiree just tripled as Embassy reinforcements streamed through the breech on their own lines.

Char ignored them. "Auri?"

"Finally found a pulse. It's faint. Real faint."

"He's been poisoned," the female contractor said. She reached toward Ben's face.

Auri snapped a cender out of his thigh holster and held the barrel against her temple. "Back off."

"Maybe you're the ones who should back off," one of the new arrivals said. He had a green tuft of hair sticking straight up out of his hat. "Contractor Efrom

Starrie and his cousin are distinguished guild members and Embassy operatives. You'll kindly lower your weapons, troopers."

"This feels familiar," Matt said. "Even down to the broken window."

Char was feeling like it was the ballroom all over again, too. "Just let us take our man and we're gone."

"He's not leaving with you," the original contractor said. "He'll be escorted to a prison cell to await trial for the murder of Liu Stavros and half of my security team."

"I assume you're the Efrom they're talking about," Char said. "And that you're in charge?"

He nodded with a self-important smile and clasped his hands behind his back.

Typical. Aiming for propriety amidst the streaks of dust and blood coating his face and the shredded clothing hanging on his limbs.

"Okay, Efrom, I'm going to give the fast and dirty version of Intra-Brazial Law 9.15.7." She looked directly into a voyeur camera. "Which exempts any military officer from trial by the hands of a civilian court while in active service. Matt, help Auri get Ben mobile. We're out of here."

Though murmurs filtered through the contractor ranks, none of them pressed the issue. Naela was surprised because she'd seen firsthand how the guild could shape a case later to justify Embassy actions. But, unlike Efrom, the newcomers had no stake in this game and would probably just as soon get the Armadans out of their way before beginning clean up.

Efrom swept a hand toward the window as if saying, "Be my guest."

But as soon as Ben's two troopers had his arms draped on their shoulders and stood with their backs to Efrom, he smirked at Naela.

"Time to pick a side, cousin." His other arm moved from behind his back.

Naela dove for Ben's rifle and fired from the floor before Efrom could get a shot off from his recovered handgun. The last round from Ben's rifle slammed into Efrom's face.

Guns spun on her from all directions and the contractor team surrounded her. But still she glimpsed Efrom fall.

She tossed the rifle away, pushed onto her knees, and laced her hands behind her head.

The green-haired contractor kicked her in the wounded shoulder, spilling her to the stone again. As he twisted her arms behind her back and slapped electronic restraints on her wrists, the pain of her injuries sent streaks of white stars into her vision.

He pulled her to her feet and marched her to the window. "You've just bought yourself a Writ of Execution."

But there were no tears for Naela to cry…out of agony or humiliation or even anger. There was a calm as she had never felt before.

Because Efrom was dead.

Where…what?

Ben heard voices near him. A woman. Two men. Maybe just one man, sometimes shouting, sometimes speaking at a regular level. He fluttered his eyelids against the bright overhead lights and finally pulled his hand up to shade his eyes.

An antiseptic mint green hospital room greeted him. Monitors beeped in the background. And an airscreen showed four well-dressed people sitting around an elaborate podium whose front transitioned through still photos of some recent event.

The Media feeds were the voices in his room. In fact, he was very much alone.

"…*Embassy can't control their own contractors, especially the assassins.*" A man Ben vaguely recognized shouted in the face of the moderator. The name bobbing in a parallelogram just below him read Archivist Harlo Andravo.

A small chuckle sounded out of the shot. The screen then filled with the source of the laughter, a beautiful blue-haired woman with delicate features. Phoebe Llewellyn, the only Quroum Archivist that at least half of the system wanted to dock.

She responded in a calm, almost hypnotic voice. "*We all seem to be forgetting that Liu Stavros wasn't exactly an innocent man—*"

"*You're awfully quick to defame the character of a dead man, Archivist Llewellyn, especially a proven businessman and philanthropic Socialite.*"

Ben missed the woman's rebuttal when he finally focused on the headline scrolling across the bottom of the podium. He wondered if he was still asleep or if the drugs the hospital gave him had hallucinogenic effects. Because what he was seeing had to be a nightmare of his own imagining.

Controversy Rages over Capture of Notorious Assassin Naela Starrie.

Her image suddenly filled the entire Media screen. His breath caught for a moment. It was an older vid, but she hadn't really changed much. Those long black tresses were blown back from her cheek and just skirted her shoulders. Her slack jaw and slightly parted lips said the camera had taken her by surprise. Only the olive skin of her face wasn't covered by shiny charcoal nylon.

Beautiful…but it wasn't *his* Naela.

The azure eyes staring from that airscreen were the wrong shade. And, it wasn't because she was using her fragger camouflage tech or because the Media likeness was off. There was no light behind those harsh eyes, no spark of the amusement he'd come to know so quickly during their time together.

Then *that* Naela vanished beneath a second image, very much like how his own image of her was evaporating. She'd been so real in his delirium as the poison was forced out of his system.

He raised his hand to trace the outline of her face on this new image, but it faded into a third. Ben kept watching as dozens of images replaced one another. None of them of the woman he had come to care about.

"Naela Starrie is getting what she deserves." Her name said so harshly on Andravo's lips brought Ben back to the debate.

The archivist continued with a sniff. *"At least Head Contractor Rainer Varden has enough sense to follow the law and decree the Writ of Execution justified."*

Ben didn't need to hear more. He pulled free from the intravenous tubing and ripped the pulse monitors from his skin. The world spun as he sat up, but he fumbled his way out of bed and to the closet. The med suite door flew open, and a nurse burst in, followed by Colin, Char, and Matt.

"What the hell are you doing?" Colin asked. "Alarms are going off all over the nurses' station."

Ben ignored his brother and searched the closet.

"I'll give you two guesses what has him riled up," Char said.

Out of the corner of his eye Ben caught her gesturing toward the latest image of Naela on the airscreen before Char extinguished it. "He kept muttering her name every time he regained consciousness on the flight here. And, it's a long flight to the Hub from Tampa Three," she added.

The nurse put a firm hand on his shoulder. "Lt. Commander, I insist—"

Ben cut her off. "I need some fu—" He took a breath. This young Socialite didn't need his attitude. He'd save that for those Embassy assholes. "I need some clothes, please." He added a smile, hoping some charm would get him out of this place sooner.

"I am responsible for your care." She didn't share his feelings about charm. "So *I need* you to get back into that bed, *please.*"

Spunky little thing, especially the way she turned his faux pleasantries around on him. Her personality reminded Ben of Mari.

Another tiny blonde who thinks she's seven feet tall. For the dozenth time he considered just how fortunate David was.

Now it was Ben's turn for a little luck.

"You don't have to be responsible," he said. "Isn't that right, Barrister Anlow?"

"By law, the patient is mobile and lucid," Colin agreed. "He can leave when he likes."

"Thank you," Ben said.

"Even if it does show off his lack of sense."

Colin always knew how to lighten the mood with his snark.

"You were the only Anlow born with any sense, so don't hold genetics against me," Ben said.

"Fine." The nurse punched something into her reporter and left.

"No goodbye?" Matt said. "You're losing your touch, sir."

"Not sure he ever had one," Char said.

"Don't know which of you is funnier. Now, is someone going to bring me some clothes? Because nobody is going to be laughing if I have to walk out of here bare-assed."

Naela tapped the wall as she paced the perimeter of her three meter by three meter holding cell for the six hundredth time in four days. Stripped down to her underwear with no shoes, movement was the only way to keep the cold at bay... and her mind occupied.

The comm station on Durstal Ki had been more inviting than this featureless synthstone box with its transparent energy field for a door. Her view was of the blindingly white wall that stretched down the hallway and out of sight. As she made another circuit past the bed and toilet, she caught some refracting shimmers from the field. An aurora on a miniature scale. The pathetic comparison was irritating.

It was always just a fantasy.

Naela thought she had prepared herself to leave the isolation, the relative safety, of Durstal Ki, but it wasn't memories of the location that inspired her disquiet—it was him.

She thought of Ben, and she hadn't *thought of* anyone in decades.

The metal entry slid open at the end of the corridor.

Meal time already?

She'd been doing so well keeping a count of time without her reporter or a wall monitor, but she obviously lost track at some point. Where was Mayfield when she needed him? She absent-mindedly wondered if they had even found his body. Then she realized she didn't really care.

Naela faced the back of her cell, palms and forehead against the chilled wall as was procedure. The snick of the energy field blinking off made her sigh. From the moment they put her in here, she'd devised several scenarios for escape, but the time had never been right. And, it had to be right because they would make sure she didn't get a second chance.

When she inhaled again, her entire body tensed.

The scent of antiseptic enveloped the space, but with it…the smell of a spiced musk she associated with only one person.

She turned her head ever so slightly, knowing even the small movement could provoke a mid-voltage shock from the overzealous gatekeepers the Embassy had assigned to watch her.

A body pressed against her back—definitely a man. His hands ground hers into the synthetic rock as he mimicked her posture from behind.

Naela threw her head back, but couldn't make contact.

"I wouldn't." Efrom's voice delivered on hot breath into her ear made the bile rise in her otherwise iron stomach. "You know what they'll do to you for even the slightest disturbance."

Part of her brain couldn't process that it was him. The horror of a defeated foe rising again to continue his torment threatened to break her psyche. There was no trick from the desert now that could bring her calm, no fragment of reality that would prove to her she was no longer that little girl smothering under the weight of his body as he took his pleasure.

He licked her ear.

She didn't move.

But a swell of rage in the far off ocean of her mind started its way to the shore of her consciousness—patient and building in intensity.

His hands moved up her arms slowly, hinting at the fondling to come.

The angry wave picked up energy from memories of her shattered childhood.

"They're going to execute you, you know."

"But just for one murder," she said, "not two. A pity."

Efrom shoved away from her.

She spun around. The sight of his normally attractive features morphed into a grotesque arrangement of spreading bruises, healing gashes, and black bandages stunned Naela. Half of his face—the half she'd shot—was covered tightly by a hood that detailed a large crater where his cheek had once been.

"Admiring your work?" he asked. "Not quite the masterpiece you made out of Stavros, but that final bullet earned me several more sessions with the reconstructive surgeon. All paid for by the money they'll pull from your frozen accounts. I admit through my own vanity that I've opted for a few extras, but you can afford it. Quite the stack of blocks you had stockpiled. I guess when you have no life besides the killing, you can get by on a modest allowance. I'll be sure to toast you on the Otherside as I enjoy the spoils."

"I may yet survive the trial," she said.

"Even if there wasn't the evidence the voyeurs recorded before the flare, my own account of the events and that of my second in command will surely sink you. And, you were wrong. You will be tried for two murders—Liu Stavros and Lt. Commander Ben Anlow."

"Ben passed?" Her grief at the news pushed the anger back in on itself as denial flooded her mind. She'd asked about him that first day, but no news of the outside world ever reached her cell.

Naela's mood swing must have caught Efrom off guard.

"What sort of fascination did you hold for that Armadan? You rebuff my advances once dear brother Nikos comes back home to save you, then you leave him for the assassin's guild. Never looking back, never asking after any of your family. But separated from Anlow for less than a week and you were already pining for him. What now? Will you sing a lamentation for his death?"

He wrapped a lock of Naela's hair around his fist. His face was just inches from hers now. She tolerated the intrusive behavior because she knew Efrom's tactics well. Her affection for Ben had shamed her cousin personally, so he attempted to bait her, even bringing up Nikos, whom he despised.

"Really, Naela." He twisted the hair tighter as he spoke. "Armadans have little more genetic purity than the Lower Caste. It's a betrayal to your heritage that you would allow an emotional fallacy for one to stain you. Can't you see that even if he had lived, it would have been only to send you to your death?"

Efrom's words were a poisoned dagger plunging into her chest...because they were true. The Embassy would have called upon Ben to give testimony. He would have tried to lie for her, but the mind scanners would expose him. The more elite contractors were only now managing to fool the biological and mental sensors from the scanners with practiced and secret techniques.

"You would have enjoyed seeing that, wouldn't you?" she asked.

Efrom rubbed his cheek against hers and whispered, "Yes. But now that he's gone...there is a way this ends well. I can secure your release. I would do that for you, for my close blood."

"And in return?"

"And in return, you marry me, swear devotion, and bear my children."

"I'm a life pledge to the assassins' guild."

"I curry favor at the highest levels of the Embassy. Arrangements could be made. You would, of course, have to remain under constant monitored security at my estate outside of Wright's Landing, but isn't living out a long life at an opulent residence preferable to the alternative?"

"A life at your mercy, at your perverted whims?" The fury churned again at the thought of Efrom as her new jailor. "I would rather die."

He yanked on her hair to pull her head to the side.

"You think death is your escape from me?" He screamed. "You think I won't have you again?"

Efrom slammed her head against the wall, then threw her to the floor. He was on top of her before she could spin around.

The first in a long line of anger-driven waves crashed inside Naela when Efrom tore at her clothes. Her body reacted without instructions from her mind. She punched him in the neck and threw him off her. Before he could regain his feet, she sunk her knee into his groin and wrapped a hand around his neck. With her other hand she ripped off the black hood and bandages to reveal pink mottled skin.

Another wave crashed.

She tore at the healing skin, ignoring his hands battering her shoulders and back. His screams brought the waves crashing faster and faster, falling in on themselves in a red maelstrom as she flayed him.

The first blast from the shockers was like a distant buzzing, a pinch to her skin. Even the initial blows from the two guards couldn't quite break into her swirling sea of destruction, but once the third contractor joined the fight, Naela started to feel every punch, every kick. Maybe it would be better to die here and now anyway rather than prolong this madness. Maybe a better life waited on the Otherside.

Her forearm snapped from a well-placed kick.

Or maybe not.

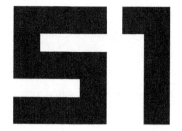

He's hesitating—not a good sign.

"I'm sorry, Ben."

Those weren't the words he wanted to hear from Colin right now.

"You went straight to Prollixer's Head Contractor?" Ben asked.

"I never spoke with Rainer Varden directly." Colin held up a hand before Ben could protest. "He's on some special assignment dealing with this ambasadora initiative. A second-in-command took one look at the names associated with the case and made it clear it was Embassy business."

"How can the Armada let this happen?" Ben asked. "They sanctioned the damn operation to bring in Stavros."

"They sanctioned *Dreadfire* to bring in Liu Stavros, not Contractor Starrie," Colin said.

"Naela. Her name is Naela."

"I understand you feel indebted to this woman—"

"Naela."

"To *Naela*," Colin said, "but neither I nor the Armada has any legal jurisdiction over this matter anymore. Since the Armada was working without full Embassy consent in the first place and since the ultimate goal of eliminating Stavros from a position where he could continue his human trafficking has been completed, they're washing their hands of the whole fiasco. Disavowing comes with the territory on most of your missions."

Ben grudgingly accepted this truth. "But shouldn't that exempt me from testimony, at least? I'm a fleet officer, for fuck's sake. The Embassy has no jurisdiction over me."

"Not usually, no, but this particular incident is a little more complicated. They've been shamed by one of their own contractors and want to make an example of her, that's all. It happens."

Ben went nose to nose with his brother. "I don't like the condescending tone, Colin. Why are you bending over for the Embassy on this one? I thought you were the best fucking barrister in the system. At least that's how you paint it for the family and all those amours you keep collecting. David was right—they snipped your balls when you took that job over an Armadan commission."

As soon as the words were out of Ben's mouth, he regretted them...mostly. His frustration with Colin's rigidity mixed with his own feelings of helplessness.

"What's going on, Ben?" Colin's voice reflected only concern. "I haven't seen you panicked since...I've never seen you panic."

Ben turned away from him, afraid the terror he felt about Naela's impending death would fill every line on his face.

"Do you have feelings for her?" Colin asked. "For Naela?"

Ben picked up his new reporter. Its silver surface shined like a mirror. In it he caught his upside down reflection and thought about what Char had said—that Naela had cut into her own flesh to hotwire her implanted reporter with the reserve chip. For him.

"Yes." No need to lie. He wasn't very good at it anyway, which was why he'd go into hiding or be arrested for contempt before testifying at Naela's trial.

"Then that changes the situation."

"Yeah, I know. It makes it worse."

"Actually," Colin said, "it makes it easier."

"How?"

"It means this is a family matter now. We can start thinking outside Intra-Brazial law. That's the Anlow motto—family above all else. And, though I may not be a soldier like the rest of you, I'm still an Anlow."

Ben snatched his brother up in a giant hug and planted a big kiss on his forehead. "Sorry I said you had no balls."

And now we're dead.

"Damn it. Damn it. Damn it." Ben flicked his emerald-hued avatar out of existence. "Again."

The rest of Dreadfire Team's avatars faded to chartreuse then white and finally pixelated. The group stretched and grumbled around the repurposed virtual gaming table. Since Auri had scavenged it from some dead fraggers in the Svetz Pods four years ago, Dreadfire had found the entertainment-style interface was the best way to strategize.

Fraggers know their tech.

"We're missing something," Ben said.

"We're missing everything," Char said. "The whole plan is terrible."

No one corrected her, even Ben.

"You know that, right?" she asked.

"It is," Ben agreed. "But I got nothing else. I think it would be better if all of you sat this one out."

"Whoa." Auri held up his hand. "When have we ever walked away from one of your plans, bad or otherwise?"

"That's the problem, isn't it?" Char swept a hand over the layout for the prison facility in the Hub. "You're trying to play it too safe. For us."

"It's not your fight," Ben said. "And, if Meke wouldn't have eavesdropped on the private discussion I was having with my brother...."

"Sounded like an argument to me," she said.

"Either way—"

"Of course we were going to help," Matt interrupted. "We get bored real easy when there's no mission."

"You get bored when there is a mission," Char corrected.

"That's why we always put you in the back of the line—no one wants to hear your mouth," Meke said.

"This coming from the woman who changes the color of her hair and nails every two days?" Matt asked.

They all stared at Meke, who had walked in as a pink-haired blonde and was now a redhead with cobalt stripes.

"I like the blue," Colin said.

"You have good taste," Meke said.

"Didn't say I didn't like it," Matt mumbled.

"I missed you guys." Ben slapped him on the back. "But Char's right. This plan sucks."

"Because you're looking at it from a military assault standpoint." Colin reset the display with a wave of his hand. "Not a legal one."

"Thought we were going illegal this time," Auri said.

"Only partially." Colin squeezed his thumb and forefinger together in the air over the center of the prison complex. It zoomed out to show a basic structure and a few surrounding buildings. "But gaining access to the prison can all stay within the letter of the law—" He tapped a finger to his avatar and one to Ben's, sliding the dark green images through the front entrance. "—if just Ben and I go in."

"So you're cutting us out too?" Char asked.

"Not at all." Colin drew a circle in the air over the rest of Dreadfire's avs and moved them to the front steps of the main Embassy building. "You'll have the most frightening assignments of all."

"You going to have us call a press conference on the Embassy steps?" Matt asked.

"That's exactly what he's thinking," Ben said. "And, it's brilliant."

"Wait. What?" Char's expression mirrored the rest of the team's. "By ourselves?"

"No," Colin said. "You'll have my second there with her Media connections to keep you company. And Xander Chu."

"Just as soon as we pluck him out of that dive he always hangs out in," Ben said.

"Oh, I volunteer to go to the Atlatl," Meke said.

"You said you'd never set foot in the place again after we went after Chu the first time," Ben said.

"I owe that asshole after he exposed our undercover op."

"I'm with Meke," Matt said.

"Sure you are." Char shared a look with Auri.

"There's still the footage of Naela shot by Stavros's private cameras and voyeurs before the flare," Colin reminded them.

"It wasn't wiped out by the radiation?" Auri asked.

"No," Ben said. "Sent directly to his personal archives off-planet."

"What about when she shot that other contractor in the face?" Char asked. "That wasn't just recorded on our voyeurs. The guilders had at least one there as well."

"There's a reason the Embassy hasn't released the footage to the Media yet," Colin said. "It's an embarrassment because it features one of their elite assassins going rogue and killing at will. But we can't depend on them keeping it to themselves once the trial begins."

"Especially," Ben added, "if they mix and paint the copy to their advantage, which is exactly what we need to do. You up for it, Auri?"

"If you can get me a copy, I can change it any way you want."

"Maybe start with a pig head on Efrom Starrie," Ben said.

"Starrie?" Char asked. "The contractor your girl shot was a family member?"

"Aren't they all?" Ben said, hoping to avoid any real discussion about a private issue. But maybe...

"I have an idea for your fictitious rendering, Auri. Let's call it a two for one special."

"I like specials," Auri said.

"Not sure I'm going to," Colin said.

"Trust me," Ben said. "Now, Auri and Char, go get your dress blues on. And make sure Javi is wearing his. The big guy is about to receive a commendation. At the Embassy Hub."

"Which just happens to be next to the impeding trial archives," Colin said.

"Rather convenient, isn't it?" Ben was already loading the archive schematics onto the gaming table. "Here's the new plan. Oh, and Char, it's a good one."

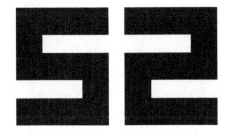

The ocean roared through Naela's ears. Though its ebb and flow was conspicuously timed with the beat of her heart.

She could barely lift her eyelids. And when she did, they fell closed again before she could make out more than a white blur.

Moving any of her limbs was impossible.

Tied down?

Stavros?!

No.

Snatches of memory invaded like brutal dreams: Stavros dead. An Armadan. Ben. Lt. Commander Ben Anlow. Pink and green auroras. Efrom. Pain.

A spike of adrenaline punched through her fugue. It was as if her eyes, her ears, and her nose opened all at once. The acrid smell of disinfectant accented the beep of a bone mender and the glare of an overhead light.

She bobbed her head to the side and noted the restraints at her wrist. A bobble to the left revealed the same and the sheen of powder blue tile covering the wall.

"You shouldn't be awake yet." A woman with tawny skin and violet braids filled Naela's view and checked on the intravenous tube sticking out of her arm. The dark green smock dress matched the doctor's large eyes.

Don't put me back under.

Naela rasped and cooed, but her thick tongue inhibited speech.

"Well," the doctor said, "since you took the effort to push right through that sedative I gave you, I suppose you deserve to have some time with your wits about you." She glanced behind her, then leaned down next to Naela's ear. "And, because you killed the animal who I believe took someone very dear to me."

Naela stopped struggling at the medic's words.

"I'd let you out of here myself if they wouldn't kill me and my family for it."

She straightened and smoothed the blanket at Naela's side. "I hope you win your freedom. Either way, you should know that there are many of us who will remember you and the justice you wrought."

She hurried out, and Naela closed her eyes again.

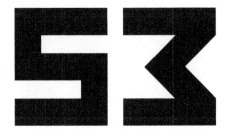

The immensity of the Embassy building here at the Hub never failed to impress Char. Stretching for two hundred hectares on multiple levels, this single structure consumed the entire right bank of Carrey Bay and dwarfed any other edifice in the system.

Spotlights and undereave illuminators lit each architecturally unique section in a specific color. None of the team spoke as the plush transport eased down the central boulevard and the government center towered above them. Its progressively changing hues and façades filled the side and roof windows beginning at the majestic main entrance. The alabaster steps and flat front reflected the aquamarine of the giant chalcedony wall that had stood sentinel inside for centuries.

The palest blues of the simplistic and stately entry gave way to deeper azure as the frontage picked up ornate details like cornices and awnings and synthstone scrollwork.

"I don't even know what is inside most of the Embassy," Char said.

"I'm not sure anyone does," Javi said, his voice still a bit rough, which only made him more attractive, in Char's opinion.

"Yeah," Auri agreed. "I heard rumors that there are sections, especially below ground, that are unmonitored and abandoned or used for secret projects."

The absurd conspiracist tale should have brought on a few chuckles from the group, but silence settled in again as the blues deepened and grotesque representations of fantastical beasts with sharp teeth and slithering tongues swept into view. The imagery, which nearly crawled off the structure as blue became purple, made Char sweat beneath the tight collar of her uniform.

Just mission nerves.

She still got them every time, no matter that she'd been in this game for decades. She learned to respect the controlled anxiety because it gave her focus, kept her sharp, and reminded her she wasn't invincible despite the cosmic luck Dreadfire had managed to date.

An audible release of breath filled the transport once the color sifted to a calming mauve and the hideous beasts transformed into abstract angles that dissipated the earlier unease.

The vehicle slowed as the traffic thickened. Pedestrians joined the mix. Many of them unconcerned with crossing at proper crossways.

A mix of grey-suited officials working late and formally clad revelers moved along the crowded walkways and spilled across the broad boulevard. The transport stopped amidst a slightly foggy sea of water vapor exhaust, crimson taillights, and beeping drivers.

Several gaggles of fashionable Socialites bumped against the group's hovering car and cackled loudly to each other as they crisscrossed to opposite sides of the street.

"Is it like this all the time?" Auri asked. He fussed with his collar as well.

"Every few hours in the entertainment district." Colin consulted his reporter. "The crowds will dissipate when the shows begin. Looks like it could be another half hour, though."

"We're going to be late," Char said. "Who's for walking?"

"Maybe we need a new plan," Javi said.

Ben clasped the big man's shoulder. "You got the easy part. Just smile pretty and say thank you when they present you with that commendation."

"I'd rather have Auri's job," Javi mumbled. "But, I'll do this for you, Ben, because you've done much worse for me."

"Thank you," he said. "Now, get out and walk. The proclamation auditorium is on the next block."

"Testing co-com," Char said once they exited the vehicle.

"Loud and clear," Ben said. *"A and O."*

As the mass of Intra-Brazial citizenry pulsed around them, Char reached down for Javi's hand. "A and O."

"Tokaki."

Efrom's face felt as though it was pressed against a hot iron. The agony erupted in full as the anesthetic medication wore off. He'd spent days in a dreamless sleep as his personal doctor kept him in a near-coma state while repairing the damage from Naela's vicious assault.

Had he witnessed her doling out this punishment on another, he would have gloried in it, been aroused by it, harbored a sense of familial pride at her strength and brutality. But she had turned her rage on him. *After* shooting him in the face in order to save the Armadan.

"Tokaki." Efrom yelled for his second-in-command because she was the only one he now trusted. Turned out the family hadn't wanted to involve itself in his ruination of Naela, even when he hinted at her involvement with Ben Anlow.

At least I had the favor of Nikos being in deep cover on some special assignment.

Otherwise, Naela's half-brother would have already killed him. Efrom was taking precautions to keep Nikos away permanently. But since his cousin had a way of surviving what the normal contractor couldn't, Efrom had at least a contingency to erase culpability from himself for Naela's execution.

And she will *be executed. No more deals.*

Any fantasies Efrom had of possessing his little cousin were torn away with his healing flesh in that jail cell.

He screamed for Tokaki again.

"Should I bring the doctor?" Tokaki stood silhouetted in the doorway.

"I just need another restor." He motioned to the table in the corner topped to overflow with garish blue bouquets of giant iridescent star lilies—a ridiculous gesture from his half-brother. "And have those vases emptied. Chen's joke is suffocating the air in here with its sweet, rotting stench."

Tokaki applied the restor patch to Efrom's neck. "Xander Chu has been located."

"I'll need another one of those," he said.

"The doctor warned against—"

"Give me another fucking restor, Tokaki."

As she peeled the backing from a second strip, he asked, "Is the team in place?"

"Yes, but there are two Armadans asking after Xander, as well."

Efrom's fingers tingled. Maybe because the double dose of restors flooded his system or maybe because….

"Give our contractors word to move on him immediately." When he made to stand, the world spun away from him. "I need a moment." He reclined again on his bed. "Tell them not to discount bringing Chu in as a corpse."

Either Efrom would use the smuggler to his own ends or at least prevent the Armadans from accessing any information he might have about Stavros, Naela, or the botanical facility.

As Tokaki made to leave, he added, "And call in a favor to double the security on the evidence room at the Hub."

Though he had tormented Naela with news that Ben Anlow was dead, Efrom had a sudden bout of paranoia concerning the man and just how far he might go to have Naela for himself.

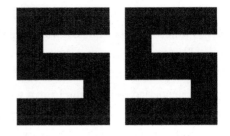

The Atlatl's familiar smell of drugs, sex, and spoiled alcohol hit Meke in the face upon being admitted to the raunchy club.

She looked beyond the blue mist of vapor drugs in search of her favorite smuggler. And, he actually was her favorite, despite what she'd led the others to believe. It was better that way, especially where Ben and Char were concerned. If Ben acted like Papa, then Char was like their Mama, though she'd clobber Meke for even thinking that, considering they were only two months apart in age.

"There." She indicated with a lift of her chin to the private elevated section in back.

"*That's* Xander Chu?" Matt shouted in Meke's ear over the intense house music thumping through the Atlatl.

"Uh hmm." From his dark shaved head down to his very cut body wrapped in blue and black leather to his booted feet crossed at the ankles and stretched far in front of him, Xander Chu exuded sex appeal more than any man she had ever met, including Colin Anlow. Even the highbrow criminal's Socialite pedigree couldn't put her off.

"I can't believe during all of our run ins with Xander you never at least caught a glimpse of him," she said.

"First of all, do you forget about the six months I was in a coma or the two separate stints I did in that orthopedic rehab facility on Tampa Deux? Second, you're chummy enough to call him *Xander?*"

"We have an understanding," Meke said.

"You seem to have a lot of those."

Meke felt a little embarrassed shock zap through her system as Matt marched away from her.

Why should you care?

He was the one who had insisted no one else find out about their trysts. He'd practically tried to bribe Auri to keep his mouth shut after the Harrigut Domes fiasco. Still, Matt had made her feel almost…guilty when she mentioned a past with Xander.

Ass.

She shook it off and whisked in front of him to take lead as they neared Xander's table where two mercs—possibly Lower Caste, though she could never really tell—barred anyone from passing into the aisle near him.

"Excuse us, gentlemen…" She slithered between them sideways. "We have an appointment with Socialite Chu."

The blondest merc moved to grab her arm, but Matt bent back the man's wrist and twisted his arm behind his back. Before the darker blond could pull his cender, Meke kneed him in the balls and strutted over to the smuggler.

One hand on her hip, she held out the other. "Got a drink for an old friend?"

"Mad, mad Meke." The way he purred her name and gave her the once-over sent betraying waves of arousal through her most intimate areas. Her gaze darted briefly to Matt, but wouldn't reach his eyes.

Xander snapped his fingers at the nearby server standing at attention. "My old friend needs a neon. You like the pink ones, if I recall."

She hated them, and he knew it from their first encounter here, before he knew she was undercover on an Armadan mission. Since then, he'd bought her one any time they happened to run into each other. It annoyed her at first, but she'd begun to associate the overly sweet, brilliantly glowing cocktail with docking Xander so they held their own sort of charm now.

"You can have one too," Xander said peeking around her to Matt. "If you let Roy go. I don't want to have to get a new bodyguard. He's finally broken in."

Matt shoved Roy aside. "We're not here for drinks."

"Didn't think so," Xander said. "Mad Meke doesn't come visit unless she needs me." He let the innuendo hang on the last word and stared pointedly at Matt.

To Meke's exhilarated surprise, Matt stepped forward to take the bait.

She put a hand on his chest and said, "This is about Ben—"

Roy pitched forward just as she felt the electric charge of a cender sizzle past.

"Down." She leapt for Xander and pulled him off his cushy chair onto the sticky carpet.

"Shit. Contractors," Xander said. "They after you?"

"Probably after you," she said.

161

"How do you know?"

"Because we're after you," Matt said.

"But not to kill you," Meke clarified.

Another blast sizzled into the table above them.

"Out the back." Xander flipped to his feet.

Matt and the other bodyguard pushed behind Meke and drove her and Xander ahead of them across the second level. Patrons looked on in curiosity at the crouching parade until a third cender shot ignited the vapor pipe in a diner's hand.

Screams and stampeding ensued.

Chaos as savior once again.

She vaulted an upturned chair and followed Xander down the steps and behind a midnight blue curtain coated in silver sparkles. Scant lighting from the cathedral ceiling far above made for careful footwork in the narrow hall. She dared a look over her shoulder, however, to spy Matt squeezing sideways through the accessway.

Before she could turn back, she plowed right into Xander.

"Oy. Watch those bony shoulders, luv. You could impale a man."

"Don't remember you ever minding before. This our stop?"

"You know it." He pushed his hand against the wall. A glow from beneath his palm indicated his reporter worked on a coded lock. Without even a click, a section of the wall cracked open.

Xander was through in a flash, obviously not concerned by the darkness that waited beyond. Meke snagged a razor disc from her pocket before she entered the abyss.

162

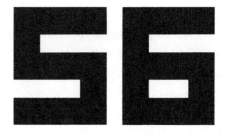

The opulent textures of blue velvet carpeting and gold pillars inlaid with real gemstones inside Shakespeare Hall were beyond intimidating. As were the expensively clothed denizens striking poses and scrutinizing the equally outrageous outfits of their counterparts.

"I feel underdressed," Javi said. "Not enough sequins or glow patches."

"The day you start wearing luminous thread is the day we have to seriously reconsider our relationship," Char said, mesmerized by the elaborate pattern of green and white lighting up the back of a Socialite man's long black coat.

"How about sequins?" Javi asked.

"How about not."

"At least it matches the guy's hair," Auri said. "What color would you call that?"

"Puke pea with a side of—"

An enthusiastic voice boomed through the gilded auditorium and cut Javi off. *"Welcome to the 7568ᵗʰ consecutive Embassy Commendation Ceremony this evening here at Shakespeare Hall. Each evening in the Tampa Quad Hub we have new citizens and some old favorites to celebrate. And tonight's show is one of the most diverse groups of awardees we've seen since…last month! So finish that champagne and find your seat. We'll be starting in ten minutes."*

"Hello there." A woman with a smile that gleamed bright white and spanned from ear to ear popped in front of the trio of soldiers. Auri actually flinched.

"Welcome. May I have your invitation, please?"

Are her eyes literally sparkling? Or maybe it was the afterglow of the puke pea jacket.

"Sergeant Javier Nikevich? We are so happy to have you as a guest with us this evening. Most of the military ceremonies broadcast in the afternoon. Not that many active duty Armadans attend." She leaned in conspiratorially. "In fact, your name had originally been left off the list until we had word from a special source—" She winked. "—that you'd be joining us. You must have done something exciting, especially to share the stage with Marion Giovani tonight. Imagine being heiress to the entire Giovani Territory *and* a vid actor. What a life."

"Exciting?" Char asked. "Yeah, he did something exciting." Her voice raised with a flash of anger at this twit's comparison of her prime to a vid actor. "Something like—"

"Thank you." Javi squeezed Char's shoulder as if to say, *It's okay.* "We're happy to be here. This is my prime Charisa Lipoli."

"Enchanted. You must be very proud."

There was only earnestness in the woman's voice. Char had missed the friendly tone before. So used to dealing with snide, vapid Socialites or openly hostile contractors had put her into defensive mode each time they went Planetside anymore. She and Javi needed a little R and R once they helped Ben out of this mess.

Her shoulders relaxed as she said, "Always proud."

Always.

"If you would please follow me to your seats, we'll begin in a few minutes. I've uploaded tonight's lengthy program to your reporters." She walked fast on teetering heels down the slight incline.

"Is there usually this much Media presence?" Auri asked in a low voice. "Or did Colin arrange this?"

"Your guess is as good as mine, considering none of us has shown up for one of these ceremonies before." Char took in the half dozen voyeurs buzzing one another just overhead to get the best camera angle.

"If we went every time one of us got a commendation for being wounded," Javi said, "we'd just have to camp out on those steps."

None of the three soldiers laughed because they knew Javi didn't really mean it as a joke. He and Auri and the rest of Dreadfire felt as Char did—the wounds never really healed, at least mentally. No matter how many limbs were reattached or new skin grown, neither the Armada nor the Embassy med facilities had found a way to eradicate the scars on the psyche.

"Here we are." The hostess swept her hand in invitation to a row in the rear of the first section. "Congratulations and enjoy." She zipped away without another word.

Javi squirmed in his seat and pulled at his collar.

"Stop fidgeting," Char said. "You look good."

And, he did. The dark indigo of the dress uniform brought out the blue specks in his hazel eyes. And the line of silver buttons down the middle of the

164

jacket reflected the bright lights of this lavish auditorium onto his face, banishing some of the pallor of his recent ordeal.

Auri scrolled through the glowing blue names on the evening's official program automatically uploaded to their wrist reporters. "You *are* in stellar company," he said. "Besides the bodacious Marion Giovani, I count two hairstylists, a fashion designer, and about sixty other recipients. Sorry I'm going to miss this."

"You can catch it on the Media reruns," Javi said.

"Just so we don't see you on any voyeur or camera streams," Char said.

"Why do you have to be physically in the room anyway?" Javi asked Auri.

"I wish you would have been at the briefing," Char said. "I'm getting tired of answering so many questions." But she smiled and bumped his shoulder. She'd answer his questions forever just to have him up and around again. "The bit syphoning machines we pulled off those fraggers in the Svetz Pods raid were only proto-types so their range isn't far."

"Ha," Auri said. "Weird coincidence that the Svetz Pods are in the Giovani Territory. You think Marion's stint as a vid actor is really a cover for her being head of the fragger organization?" Amusement tugged at the corner of his mouth. "I'd volunteer to question her, if it came down to it."

"Right after you acquire some sensitive material for our intrepid leader," Char said. "Which will be even more of a challenge since the Embassy upped security after a bit syphon attempt at Palomin."

"Someone tried to steal data from the archive reserves?" Javi asked.

"And, during a suicide party for the Sovereign's nephew, no less." Char missed gossiping like this with her prime.

"That's more ballsy than what we're doing."

"Oh yeah? Tell me that again once I'm out safe and sound. We have a very short window to erase that data. Heading in," Auri said.

"A and O," Char and Javi said together, flashing their fire ring tattoos in a fisted salute.

Soon. Soon.

Ben and Colin sauntered through the sharp angled archway of glass and into the Embassy prison facility. Only capital criminals earned a stay at the Hub. Ben had never set foot in the place until now, though he'd heard stories of just as many innocent citizens disappearing inside these glittering white calcite walls as legitimate suspects.

He took solace in the high Media profile associated with the Stavros case—whether it offered true protection for Naela's safety remained wishful thinking. If the Sovereign did indeed have a horse in this race, all bets were off.

Another thought caught Ben off guard. He halted Colin with a hand around his forearm. "What if they recognize me? There's been a shitload of coverage on the Oracle Boards, and even though the Armada's been doing a good job of keeping most of our faces out of the spotlight, I've seen myself on the screens a few times."

"Relax. This may be a highly secure facility, but it doesn't mean the contractors here know anything about the case. Play it confidently and there won't be a problem. Now straighten your lapel. It's like you've never worn a tunic suit before."

"Only when Mum made me." Ben tugged at the tailored jacket and ignored the sweat already beading at his hairline.

A contractor duo intercepted the Anlow brothers before they even reached the security kiosk. A female with long black hair stepped into their path. She gripped a cender at her side.

Ben marveled at how much she looked like Naela, especially around the eyes.

"Visiting hours are over." The high-pitched voice broke the spell and had him noticing all the flaws in her appearance. At least they were flaws in his opinion because they no longer reminded him of Naela.

"I'm Barrister Colin Anlow and I have court permission to see my client whenever I choose." Colin flipped open an airscreen from his reporter and presented the document Auri had modified from Colin's real stock of official memorandums.

The contractor scanned the virtual text with her reporter. Her partner hung back at the kiosk. A long red braid slithered down the front of her shiny black uniform and ended just above the hilt of her unholstered weapon.

"The prisoner is no longer in that cell," the brunette said.

"What?" Ben asked. "Where the hell is she?"

"Transferred from the infirmary ward to a high-level security cell."

"Infirmary? What happened to her?" Ben stepped toward the contractor guard, who raised her gun in response.

Colin placated his brother with a raised finger. "As her council I should have been informed—"

"Tell me," she interrupted, "does an Armadan barrister like you get off on representing a contractor traitor? Or do you just need the money?"

"You're violating a half dozen Embassy laws by keeping me from my client." Colin wouldn't take the bait.

But Ben wanted blood. "Let's say we skip all the law stuff and see what you've got without the Embassy behind you."

"Lt. Commander, you need to stand down." Colin's use of military-speak irritated Ben more, but it did snap him into soldier mode.

"What is his purpose here?" she asked.

"He is my assistant," Colin said. "Now, please direct us to Contractor Starrie's new cell before I have to call the Justice Quorum and we both have too much paperwork to occupy our time."

The threat of mind-numbing bureaucratic data shuffling inspired cooperation. She tapped her palm. A map pixelated over Colin's airscreen. A pulsing blue light striped over the soft mauve of the glowing map to trace a route to the high security ward several levels below ground.

"Thank you." Colin minimized the screen to his palm.

Ben was already headed for the elevator bank. As he passed through the full body scan at the kiosk, the redhead followed him.

"I'll escort you so you don't get lost." She swiped her reporter over the elevator controls to activate them. The large triangular buttons flashed green. "You'd be surprised how many people we've lost down there."

The hum of an ascending car sounded behind the steel doors, but the noise in Ben's mind nearly drowned it out. He ran through scenario after scenario to adjust to the intrusion of the escort and what he might find when they reached Naela. So far nothing was going to plan. He hoped the others were having better luck on their ends...or he might have fucked them all.

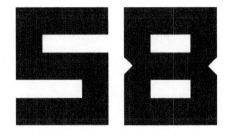

The stale beer and piss smell was starting to get to Meke. "Where does this lead?" she asked after half an hour of stomping through the dark hallway.

"To Latullip Underground," Xander said. "And my ship."

"We can't go to the underground." Meke stopped him with a tug on his arm. "Why?"

"Because," Matt spoke up. "We have to get you to the steps of Shakespeare Hall within the hour. You have a date with a Media agent."

A huge bang sounded at the corridor's entrance.

"Guess my secret escape route isn't so secret anymore," Xander said. "Shit, Meke, whatever you're planning, I'm out."

She pressed a high-dose restor into his neck before he could sprint off. His body didn't quite collapse to the floor due to the narrow space.

The hairs on her arm stood up, warning of the static blast of a cender. Its crackling white-blue trail streaked through the dark space, but the contractor had aimed high. Even Matt and the merc could squat down far enough to escape all but the residual energy from the shot.

Before the bodyguard could fire back a blast of his own, Matt pushed in front of him. "I got this." He rolled a flash grenade toward their pursuers. "Flash out."

Meke hid her face in Xander's chest. His scentbots made him smell of blue skies and turquoise oceans, much better than the reek of this passageway. The pop of the grenade was subtle compared to the visual wave of searing white blindness it released upon the confined area. Meke saw stars and black dots even with the extra cover from Xander's body.

Matt must have been affected more than expected, too. She could hear him and sort of saw a blurry form of what she assumed was him barrel down the hallway and bump into the walls more than once. The bodyguard made the mistake of following Matt down. The man may have been trained for action like this once upon a time, but he had obviously never dealt with combat tactics. He ran right into the hot end of a cender and lost his head—or the top of it anyway.

As Meke's vision sharpened, she drew her razor discs and let two fly in rapid succession into the merc's executioner. Matt had already dispatched the second contractor.

He walked back with his arm against a wall for a guide.

"You good?" she asked.

"A little bruised, a little bloody."

"Fantastic. Now, help me drag Xander out of this claustrophobic nightmare."

"That will be the easy part." Matt pulled one of Xander's arms over his shoulder and side-stepped back the way they had come.

"Clearing the three bodies in our path will be the hard part?"

"No." Matt adjusted his grip on Xander, banging the smuggler's head against the wall.

Meke caught a smile dance across her partner's face.

"The hard part will be getting him through the bar district to a transport without a voyeur noticing."

He was right. The contractors were sure to be monitoring the little flying spies in this area for any sign of Xander now that they had sent a team in.

"I got this," she said, mocking his tone earlier. "But Xander's going to be pretty pissed when he wakes up."

"It already sounds like a perfect plan."

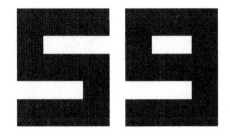

Char and Javi stood with the rest of the audience in ovation to Philanthropist Fu Sherridan even as the show's producers played over the last of his speech about the plight of Lower Caste children and the Embassy's shameful ignorance of the problem.

"I hope he has an armed escort out of the Hub," Javi said. "Because the powers that be aren't going to like talk of giving the Lowers a helping hand, children or not."

"They'll wait until the public adoration subsides," Char said. "Then he'll just disappear, probably into the same prison Ben and his brother are breaking into right now."

The host returned with a joke that fell flat on the heels of such an outpouring of legitimate emotion.

Flummoxed, he gaped for a moment then drew the crowd back to his favor when he said, "Now, distinguished guests, we have the honor to recognize a truly great actor and dramatist. Please welcome the stylish and incomparable Marion Giovani to the stage for her outstanding performance on last night's episode of *Dangeroux*."

The cameras swarmed the ultra-glamorous starlet three sections over. She glided to the stage in a silky sapphire gown with a trail so long it took three attendants to man it, plus an extra one just for her lengthy onyx bejeweled locks. Amidst the uproarious applause, Char's reporter buzzed against her wrist.

"Auri's run into extra security. Either our informants were off or Efrom Starrie is suspicious of tampering."

"Do we go after Auri?" Javi asked.

That had been her first instinct, too, but blowing his cover was a last resort.

"You're just trying to get out of this commendation. Seriously, he'll let us know if he needs us. You know Auri—he's as resourceful as he is pretty."

"Then we're in trouble. Because I always thought he was one ugly son of a bitch."

"I'm so glad you're back." She straightened a pin on his uniform. "Now look sufficiently modest, but proud, because you're up right after the stylist who came up with Marion's look tonight. Half the system will be spending their day tomorrow trying to grow more hair."

Char's reporter buzzed again, but she didn't have a chance to check it before Auri broke radio silence in her co-com.

"Shit. Trapped. Need a distraction for about six voyeurs."

The feed clicked off. She didn't dare answer him. The Embassy scanners may have already picked up on Auri's transmission, especially if they noted his bit syphoner drawing from their evidence archives.

"You get that?" Char asked Javi.

"Yep. Let's break in there and get him."

"I have a better idea. We'll make them come to us."

As they rushed up the aisle, Javi said, "So, is your plan going to be more painful than getting up on that stage in front of all these people?"

"Definitely."

Just as they exited the double leaded glass doors at the back of the auditorium, the announcer said, "Welcome Sargeant Javier Nikevich."

"I can't wait," Javi said.

Do I take her out now? Probably still need her in case the map doesn't lead to Naela.

The elevator slowed and opened. The car's interior had been conspicuously devoid of floor numbers—maybe how so many visitors got lost—so Ben had no idea as to the depth of their descent.

Four gleaming white commonways starbursted from the elevator bank and reminded Ben of that similar configuration at Durstal Ki. A pang of longing pressed his chest. He wanted to go back to that remote mountain greenhouse. Just Naela and him. No Mayfield. No venomous pumas. And no Efrom.

"This way." The contractor female motioned to the far left corridor.

Ben ticked off the steps of his plan as a meditation. Much of it relied on circumstances beyond his control, but he had faith in his team. And in his family. He drew strength from Colin's presence. More than at any other moment, Ben now understood that their joke about Colin being a legal warrior wasn't hyperbolic. The battle for Naela's freedom, for her life, rested in his hands. Ben may as well have been decoration at this stage.

Irritation and frustration destroyed his meditation.

The featureless commonway stretched on interminably until it finally took a dogleg to the left. Empty cell after empty cell witnessed their passing. After a dozen of these doorless alcoves—with at least a dozen more reaching into the distance—he caught the hazy edge of an energy field coming up on the right.

Behind the iridescent sheen of a "live" door stood Naela. She'd obviously heard their approach and was standing ready, as if she expected a fight.

He couldn't say anything as he looked her over. His imagination played out horrible scenarios about how she may have gotten her injuries. Bruises, a bloodshot eye, a swollen lip, a bone mender circling one arm. Someone had done this to her while she was locked away in here.

Alone.

While I slept off a poisoned binge.

He couldn't see past vengeance and rage…until she spoke his name.

"Ben?" Her tone sang with relief and anticipation. "How can this be?"

The tension drained so quickly from his body that he thought his knees would buckle.

"Nalea, baby. Imagine running into you here." His speech betrayed him with its emotional rasp.

Colin shifted next to him, and the contractor let out a condescending little sound, as though hearing the intimacy between Naela and an Armadan fouled the redhead's sense of propriety.

"Efrom told me—" Her voice caught, but she recovered into the stone façade she'd had when he first followed her over the bow of Stavros's fortress. "I was led to believe you were dead."

"A little bad drink hasn't kept me down before." Then he spoke to the contractor hovering beside him. "Can we please have some privacy?"

She snorted. "This is a maximum security prison. Nothing is private here." She pointed out cameras flush against the ceiling and walls. They were so well camouflaged that he couldn't look at them directly, but rather only catch their white glint out of the corner of his eye.

For good measure, a voyeur floated down the corridor behind them. Its eerie all-seeing lenses snapped open and closed with hungry metallic snaps—for some in the Intra-Brazial, these observers were the ultimate tormentors.

"Embassy regulations allow for unattended meetings between a client and barrister," Colin said.

Before she could argue, he said, "But since there are mechanical witnesses in abundance…" He looked directly into the closest camera. "…I formally request you take leave of us."

She didn't look happy about the one-upping with the oldest voyeur trick in the book, but relented. "Fine. But if I go, he goes, too."

"He's necessary to my work—"

"Bullshit. He's no more your assistant than I am. I need to see credentials before he stays."

Colin flashed his palm screen at her.

Ben looked at Naela, who had remained still and quiet, as if she didn't trust he was actually standing there. "This is all going to work out."

As if to confirm his statement, the redhead said without further provocation, "I'll be just around the corner if you need me." She pulled her fingers away from Colin's open screen.

Ben caught the site of a money transfer before the display faded from Colin's hand.

"Ben, there's noth—" Naela began, but he silenced her with a finger to his lips before pulling one of Auri's toys from his pocket.

What would have looked like a blue currency block to the security scanners was actually a basic virtual scarecrow. He depressed one end of the block and waited for it to turn purple as it sent a video looping program to the cameras and voyeurs within eyeshot.

"We probably have ten minutes until the program is discovered," Ben said. "Until then it will show the same minute of footage continuously."

"Audio?" Naela asked.

"There won't be any audio, so let's hope no one is listening to the live feed."

"It's good to see you." She stepped so close to the electric field that her hair frizzed on the ends. "But there's nothing you can do."

"Maybe not, but he can. Naela, meet my brother, Colin, barrister extraordinaire."

A smile broke the severity of her expression and puffed her swollen lip out farther. "I think I'm past the lawyer phase after practically flaying Efrom in my last cell."

"Did you kill him?" Ben hoped she had because the fucker deserved it, but also hoped the answer was no because their plan hadn't accounted for an extra murder charge.

"The guards...*subdued* me first."

"Even beat up, you're still the most beautiful woman in this system."

"As much as I'm enjoying seeing my little brother swoon," Colin said. "We have a lot to talk about and not much time."

"You have a plan?" Naela asked.

"Three, to be exact," Ben said.

"Three?" she asked.

"A guy's got to be prepared."

"Let's hope it doesn't come down to that third one." Colin looked at Naela. "I don't think you're going to like it."

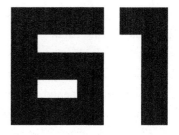

As soon as Char and Javi hit the grey and lavender marble lobby, she started to shout. "Fu Sherridan. There's been an attempt on Fu Sherridan. Armed men. In masks."

"Masks?" Javi asked.

"Overdoing it a bit?"

Voyeurs closed in from every direction. "Guess not. 'Cause it's working." Javi's words were tight as his body already tensed under the scrutiny.

"Come on. We need to pull them outside with us." Char ran toward the main entrance as though she really were in pursuit of armed men in masks.

The airborne balls of cameras and mics trailed behind the Armadan couple and alerted the Media crew waiting on the steps.

The contractor guards at the entry made to intercept, but Donna Lichten, Colin's second amour, had her Media personnel shoving into the doors and giving the contractors other concerns. The investigative journalist played along with the new plan, sensing either Dreadfire's need for improvisation or just a better story for her show that evening.

Char hoped her and Javi's antics would provide spark enough to light the Oracle Board fuses and give Auri the cover he needed.

When they pushed onto the main Embassy steps, it was obvious to Char that Donna's crew only feigned an attempt to breach the entry—their extra lighting was still set up on the hand-carved stairs where Dreadfire was meant to give a statement about the Naela Starrie case after the ceremony.

So much for the 'planned' ambush.

But Donna played her role well by rushing at Char with questions and three voyeurs orbiting her. "Did you say Philanthropist Fu Sherridan is in danger? Was it an attempt on his life? What kinds of masks were the assailants wearing?"

Before Char could speak, the fair-haired Donna looked into the closest lens and addressed her audience of millions. "I'm here on the beautiful steps of Shakespeare Hall with…excuse me, what is your name?"

The middle voyeur swooped down close to Char's face, and she nearly batted it out of the air. "Char."

Donna waited for more, then picked up the beat again once she saw Char's irritated expression. "Char, can you tell us what you saw? What happened to Fu Sherridan?"

"Nothing happened to me."

They all spun around to face Sherridan and his well-armed entourage.

Shit. Hadn't expected anyone to see through the lie until tomorrow, at least.

"Um," Char said.

Donna's nose twitched in agitation, but she was used to putting people on the spot. "Fu Sherridan, we had word that you were under attack. How do you explain your escape?"

"My what?" He searched the faces of everyone standing around him, which now numbered in the low sixties as passersby flitted over to be part of the show.

Donna never missed an opportunity to confuse the situation further and take the heat off the Armadans. "Do you believe the Embassy was trying to retaliate for your remarks this evening about the government's neglect of Lower Caste children?"

That got his attention. His gaze darted around the burgeoning crowd as though he did expect masked gunmen at any moment. The half dozen mercs he'd arrived with circled him and kept their hands on concealed weapons.

The hypocrisy of letting non-military Armadans carry guns Planetside chafed, but the paranoia Donna was inspiring worked.

She dove in with another question about any other recent attempts on his life when Char's reporter buzzed again.

Not Auri, but Ben.

His message blinked in urgent blue neon: *Evidence destroyed?*

She debated for a moment whether to use the co-com again. Javi must have read her mind as he had Ben's message. A gentle shake of his head said it all. They couldn't risk giving up Auri's position.

She tried him on his reporter instead. Seconds ticked by.

Ben's message repeated.

Unknown, she sent back. It stung to admit they may have failed him. When his next message came through, though, she knew it would be like sticking a knife through his heart with her answer.

But Xander Chu is ready?

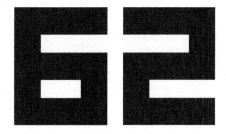

Patience. It's not over yet.

Ben checked the countdown on his reporter. It now tallied up in red. "Two minutes past looping."

"Plan one?" Colin asked, referring to the evidence destruction.

"Still in progress."

"And plan two is obviously stalled." He opened an airscreen to show his second browbeating a man who was definitely not Xander Chu, while Char and Javi looked around anxiously in the background.

A warning beep sounded from the looper.

"We've been made." Ben looked at Colin. "Can't wait any longer. Last resort."

"It can't be that bad," Naela said. "Our previous last resort plan got you out alive."

"And, now I'm returning the favor. Naela Starrie, will you marry me and let me save you?"

This should have been more of a moral dilemma for Ben because his decision was based as much in passion as logic. And it took the counsel of a brother he hadn't ever really felt close to in order to convince Ben to trust his emotions—a shocking idea coming from a multi-amoured man in a society where emotional fallacies were pariahs.

"What?" Naela asked.

Colin spoke up. "Amours, by law, cannot testify against each other."

"No," she said.

Her sudden rejection cut Ben deeper than he had anticipated. Maybe he had naively expected her to say yes, to share his passion, at least for her own life. "It doesn't have to mean anything—"

"But it means everything," she said. "I didn't save your life on that mountain only for you to throw it away on a forced marriage."

"They will *force* me to testify against you, Naela. I would swear your innocence until my death, but I can't beat the lie detectors in that courtroom. No matter how much I would want to, Armadans just can't seem to fool the sensors. If I testify, you lose…everything."

"No," she said again.

Naela's heart pounded so hard that she mistook its beating for the clomping of boots running from the connecting commonway.

"Go," she said, "before they get here."

But Ben remained rooted to the spot. The lines on his face betrayed a deep hurt.

He stepped as close to the field as he dared…then surprised her with a smile. She liked his smile. When meant for her, it was exhilarating. Almost like fighting for her life, only it was quite the opposite. Ben's smile reminded her she was alive, if only for a little while longer.

"Sorry," he said. "But I will not let you die because of me. A and O." He pulled out a device she recognized as a fragger disruptor. Before she fully realized he meant to dampen the cell's energy, he grabbed her arm and yanked it through the field. Electricity poured through both of them.

Naela struggled, but Ben held on tight.

"You'll just have to hate me for the rest of your life. But at least you'll have your life."

Colin snapped the sampler onto her forearm and mixed her blood with Ben's in a unity vial. Holding it high in the air, for the cameras to see, he announced, "Amours brought together until death. As a legal barrister of the Embassy, I, Colin Anlow, officially record this marriage into the Intra-Brazial archives for all eternity. Let the Tradition and the law stand."

The booted feet rounded the doglegged corner. Contractors shouted orders. "Move away from the cell. Hands behind your head."

Security voyeurs surrounded the scene.

Efrom pushed through the initial guards, then faltered in his step when he saw the blood vial shimmering in Colin's hand.

"Lieutenant Commander Anlow," Efrom said without taking his focus from the vial. "You are detained for illegal visitation of an echo level prisoner." Efrom stared Colin in the eye. "And, your barrister can join you as an accomplice."

Colin tucked the vial inside his lapel and opened an airscreen. "This is now a supervised conjugal visit between Lt. Anlow and his prime in accordance with Embassy Statute 8.16."

"You don't really think this sham of a wedding will pass in court," Efrom said.

No one else in the room but Naela could probably recognize the doubt behind her cousin's confident words.

"It's quite obvious this is an attempt to undermine the judicial system with a fake marriage of convenience."

"On the contrary," Colin said. "These two Intra-Brazial citizens were legally joined according to the Tradition."

"Not until the blood exchange is signed." The confidence in Efrom's voice was real this time as he gestured toward the unsigned document hanging in the air.

Ben tapped open a palm screen and scribbled an electronic signature onto the document with his middle finger. His name in big, bold letters appeared on Colin's airscreen as he wrote. He presented his palm to Naela who simply stared at the glowing blue display.

Efrom snorted in triumph. "You underestimated her duty to tradition and family."

Even in combat Ben had never felt so panicked. "Naela, baby, you have to sign this. Please."

"My dear little cousin and I have made our own arrangements," Efrom said.

"Judging by that black hood covering most of your ugly face, I'd say she turned you down."

"Tokaki, Willa, arrest these men," Efrom ordered.

"Naela," Ben urged.

Colin leaned in to whisper in Ben's ear, but faced Naela. When he spoke, Ben understood that Colin had wanted Naela to read his lips. "If she doesn't sign it, I can't save you from this one. You're likely to follow her to the execution chamber."

The light, frantic touch of Naela scrolling her finger along Ben's palm brought a rush of exhilaration through his system. His gaze searched her expression for a hint of her emotion. Nothing, not even when she hesitated once before completing her signature.

With the last swoop of her finger, Ben pulled his hand away and pointed at the airscreen. "Look for yourself. Naela St...." His gaze met hers. "Naela Anlow."

While Ben and Colin exchanged stunned looks, Efrom flew into a rage.

"You would forsake our kind, our family, our *name*, and offer pathetic submission to..." Efrom's voice rang loud. "To *anyone*, let alone a brute of an Armadan?"

He lunged at her, knife drawn.

"Get the fuck away from my prime." Ben slid between Efrom and Naela. Efrom bounced off the larger man's chest and stumbled back.

When he made a swipe for Ben's face, it ended with Ben grabbing Efrom's arm and forcing the blade from his grasp.

"You want to battle, asshole?" Ben twisted the contractor's arm again.

The other contractors had their guns at the ready along their sides, but knew better than to draw just yet. The two prison guards took position in front of Naela. Efrom's team rallied beside him.

"Ben," Colin warned.

Efrom shook out of Ben's grasp and in a rage aimed his cenders. Weapons alarms blared through the entire floor. The voyeurs took up position around Efrom with a snapping of telescoping cameras.

What no one saw, but they all knew lurked in camouflaged hiding were automatic plasma rifles sited in on the current threat—Efrom.

He lowered his guns and pulled a deep breath. Though he pretended to compose himself, his limbs shook in anger. "You will still be executed for crimes against the Embassy, cousin. I have visual and audio evidence showing you killing an Intra-Brazial citizen of high merit. And another key witness—one you won't have time to marry before the court proceedings."

"Actually," Colin said, "you're probably going to want to see this." He augmented the airscreen until it took up the entire space behind him.

Donna and her Media crew huddled around Char and Javi—who was looking a hell of a lot better—on the steps of the Embassy.

"That's my family," Ben said, "and they're all giving their statements right now, publicly."

A familiar face peered up from the edge of the swirling crowd. Matt, standing taller than most of the Socialites around him, led Meke and….Ben actually laughed out loud at Xander Chu's makeover.

No doubt thanks to Meke.

"You recognize that Socialite piece of shit right there?" Ben pointed to the bottom of the screen to a mop of bright blue hair.

The pupil of Efrom's good eye dilated with anxiety as the blue haired smuggler followed in Matt's wake toward the press conference.

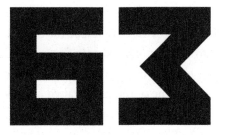

Meke sneezed from the mixture of expensive—and some not so expensive—perfumes, scentbots, and colognes wafting from the crowd. She swore the combination made a hazy cloud above their heads.

"Char and Javi are ahead," Matt said. "Looks like Colin's second has her hooks into an Embassy official now. The guy's terrified."

Meke picked up the conversation between the journalist and the official firsthand but also echoed from a half dozen Media screens floating high above within the immediate vicinity.

"Was this an elaborate scheme by the Embassy to assassinate one of its citizens?" Donna asked. "Like the attempt on Fu Sherridan tonight?"

"On the contrary," the official said. "The Embassy wanted to save Liu Stavros."

"So, you deny sending Contractor Naela Starrie?"

"Of cour—"

"Even though I have a copy of the order from notable persons high within the government not only authorizing her to infiltrate Liu Stavros's residence on Durstal Ki, but to investigate her cousin, Efrom Starrie? Or was she there to save Socialite Stavros from his head contractor?"

"I don't know where you're getting your sources." The official made to leave, but the crowd squeezed him back into the Media spotlight.

"So, that isn't a denial?" Donna asked.

Those gathered hushed in anticipation of his response.

"No comment."

But the journalist was like a cat with a toy. "Then will you comment on the Armadan team lead by Lt. Commander Ben Anlow that was purportedly sent in as a cleanup crew in case of an outcome quite like the one which played out on top of that mountain?"

"No comment." The official raised his hand and called for security again.

"Last question." Donna spit out as a small force of contractors was parting the crowd by force to rescue the official. "Isn't it true that the Embassy used Naela Starrie as a scapegoat once Stavros fell?"

The contractors breeched the wall of gawkers encircling Donna's crew and the official. One of the males raised a cender to her company's voyeur.

"It is true," came a voice from the crowd. "I have proof."

Xander Chu stepped forward with Meke and Matt.

"About time," Char said. At least part of this team came through.

"Where's your proof?" Donna yelled and gestured wildly for her crew to drag the newcomer closer.

"Right here." Xander held up his hand.

The giant Media screens all stuttered out.

"Wait. That's not what I—"

Meke elbowed Xander in the ribs, shutting him up.

"I have a feeling this is going to be better," she said.

Char waited in the glow of her reporter's palm screen like the rest of the crowd, except hers and Javi's lit up with a message from Auri. *No go on evidence. But had a mix and paint ready to go. Enjoy.*

Within seconds, the Media screens crackled back to life. Efrom Starrie's image loomed overhead, accompanied by a pounding beat and odd electronic....

"Is that a cow mooing?" Char asked.

"Not sure, but I know I heard a pig that time."

The driving club music, punctuated with its mocking animal calls, was a hit with the crowd, and drew even more observers. Or maybe it was the various images of Efrom Starrie in situations so debasing that, even when they were proven to be fake, would always be a part of the man's legacy.

"Auri better make sure his electronic prints smear," Javi shouted at Char. "'Cause this is going to bring on some shit."

Leave it to their unofficial mech tech to go off-script.

The last image of Efrom faded with the music's intensity. A jaunty melody kicked up in direct contrast to the gravity of what now showed on the screen. An official Embassy document slowly scrolled down the display—a Writ of Execution for Liu Stavros for crimes against Intra-Brazial citizens. The recipient was Contractor Naela Starrie.

"Good forge job there," Javi muttered.

"Auri's good," Char agreed.

A voiceover joined the music until both the song and the scrolling document gave way to a vid.

"Shit, Meke," Xander said. "You didn't say my private vid was going to be broadcast over the Oracle Boards."

"I actually didn't know what Auri had planned," Meke looked innocently at Char.

"Me neither," she said to Xander. "He's kind of a loose cannon."

"Hey, there you are," Matt said. "Minus the blue hair." He snickered.

"Yeah, we'll talk about that later," Xander said.

On the big screens Xander stood by an egg-shaped ship. He continued to speak to someone off-camera. *"You can promise me amnesty from any Embassy repercussions?"*

The scene jumped to Naela, and an audible gasp surfed the crowd. *"You'll probably receive a commendation for your cooperation in this sensitive mission. At the very least a pardon for your past indiscretions."*

His expression looked skeptical. *"Why are they sending you in when they have contractors already installed in this facility?"*

"Because the Embassy believes they can no longer count on the loyalty of certain members of that particular group."

The image flipped back to Efrom.

Got you, fucker.

Efrom was already backing down the hallway. "It will be exposed as lies."

On screen, Donna resumed her station front and center of the camera and asked the rattled Embassy official, *"I'll ask you again. Was Naela Starrie actually on an undercover mission for the Embassy as that vid and documentation we just saw proved?"*

The crowd turned agitated, calling for Naela's release and Efrom's head. They closed in.

The official's brow beaded with sweat. He cleared his throat and spoke loud and clear, *"Contractor Naela Starrie did fulfill a writ sanctioned by the Embassy. She was already being released before this Media fiasco once the authorities were apprised of the situation."*

"And what of Contractor Efrom Starrie?" Donna asked.

The official wiped his face with a handkerchief.

"Sir?"

The crowd murmured louder, some calling for the *official's* head now.

"He's being detained. I have no further comments."

The guards stepped away from Naela. "Guess you're free to go," the redhead said, then directed her attention to Efrom. "You, on the other hand...."

"Just got fucked," Naela said.

Efrom flipped his cender up, but amidst the blaring warning of the security system, one of the females nearest him smashed him over the head with the butt of her own weapon.

He collapsed and both women from his team were on him, getting in dirty shots at every turn in their attempts to subdue him.

After a swift kick to the balls, the taller one grabbed him by the black hood and said, "I'm glad you gave me time to think about *your* proposal because I'm really looking forward to testifying against you."

"Tokaki," he screamed.

The other woman spoke. "You're not going to testify against him. And neither am I."

Efrom played up to her, nearly groveling. "Willa, my dear, you were always the brightest of my protégés." When he reached a hand for her, she walked away from him, then spoke to both guards. "Should Contractor Starrie find himself 'disappeared' into one of these labyrinthine cells, I believe *you'll* find yourselves much wealthier."

She turned and addressed Naela and the Armadans. "Unless there are any objections."

"Lost and forgotten, rotting away never to be heard from again?" Ben shared a look with Colin. "Objections, counselor?"

"None."

"Naela?" Ben asked. "Any last words for your cousin?"

"What cousin?" she asked.

"Yet again you turn your back on your family—"

The one named Tokaki kicked the still-kneeling contractor in the face, rendering him unconscious.

"Grab a leg, Willa." Together they dragged the man down the hallway.

The redheaded guard gave Ben and the others one last look before saying, "You need an escort out?"

Ben flipped open an airscreen. "Still got my map."

He was stalling. Now that this was all over, now that his impossible plan actually worked out, he had to face Naela.

The ever-observant Colin patted Ben's shoulder and said, "I'll meet you topside."

With nothing more to use as a distraction, Ben had to face the woman he'd forced into being his prime. They caught each other's gazes. He saw in hers the same timidity and uncertainty that he felt. Without speaking a syllable, he knew she was thinking the same thing—*now what?*

For a man who could never keep his mouth shut, he found himself unable to respond.

It was Naela who was brave enough to answer for both of them…with the touch of her lips to his.

She was always the braver one.

And, Ben was humbled by her.

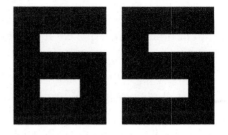

The bustling morning soundtrack of the Hub played in Naela's ears as she and Ben walked down the steps of the Embassy. Engines roared from space craft and inter-atmosphere shuttles streaking past or rising above the shining water of Carrey Bay into the bright sky above. The entire bay bubbled with boats of all sizes transporting citizens as far as the eye could see.

Chattering voices and music and general cacophony rose from passersby and the giant Media screens, which hovered at every vantage and showed a thousand different channels.

"I miss the quiet," she said. "And the aurora."

"I miss a lot of things about that mountain. Seemed safer there."

"Because my family saw fit to put a death bounty on my head? Or because the Embassy 'excused' me from duty with the warning that my past would eventually catch up with me?"

"Pretty much both."

"Close your eyes." She already had as she took his hand and shut out the organized chaos of this place in favor of another far away.

"Can you see that blinding wave of green and pink light shimmering across the night sky and among the peaks of Chumbal Range?"

"Yes, I can," he said. "And it's nearly as beautiful as my new prime."

His hand curling around hers as an anchor sent emotion radiating through her chest. They were silent then and simply basked in the scene…and in each other's comforting presence.

About the Author

Heidi Ruby Miller uses research for her stories as an excuse to roam the globe. With degrees in Anthropology, Geography, Foreign Languages, and Writing, she knew early that penning fast-paced, exotic adventures would be her life. She's put her experiences and studies to paper in her far-future Ambasadora series and into her two new thriller series.

In between trips, Heidi teaches creative writing at Seton Hill University, where she graduated from their renowned Writing Popular Fiction Graduate Program the same month she appeared on *Who Wants To Be A Millionaire*. *Ambasadora* was her thesis novel there, and the multi-award winning writing guide *Many Genres, One Craft*, which she co-edited with Michael A. Arnzen, is based on the Seton Hill program and was named #5 in *The Writer* magazine's Ten Most Terrific Writing Books of 2011.

She has had various fiction and non-fiction publications, as well as various jobs, including contract archaeologist, foreign currency exchanger at Walt Disney World, foreign language teacher, and educational marketing director for Frank Lloyd Wright's House on Kentuck Knob. In 2012, Heidi created the Dog Star Books science fiction imprint for Raw Dog Screaming Press and was the managing editor for the line for three years. Recently she was the Director of Professional Writing Relations for the Pennsylvania Literary Festival, an event she co-founded in 2014.

Her formal memberships include The Authors Guild, International Thriller Writers, Pennwriters, Littsburgh, and Science Fiction Poetry Association. She is fond of high-heeled shoes, action movies, chocolate, and tea of any sort. Heidi lives near Pittsburgh with her award-winning writer husband, Jason Jack Miller, and a sweet little kitty.

THE PLANETS OF THE AMBASADORA-VERSE

TAMPA ONE

The first to be terraformed, Tampa One was only halfway settled before its larger neighbor, Tampa Deux, was ready for habitation. Home to large swaths of unspoiled wilderness, like Archenzon, much of the moon remains a preserve for millions of species of animal and plant life.

TAMPA DEUX

Heavily populated, even after Tampa Three was terraformed, Tampa Deux's popularity still grows because of its infrastructure and planning.

TAMPA THREE

The smallest of all the moons, it was originally meant to be an exclusive world for Socialite families with the most money; however, bad terraforming and rushed planning made this the least desirable in the system.

YURAI

This world was terraformed to compete with Tampa Three as the optimal planet. Socialites left it to the Armadans because they believed its potential wasn't as high as Tampa Three, but now Yurai's size and wealth is rivaled only by Tampa Quad.

TAMPA QUAD

The most populated planet in the system, Tampa Quad is the center of government and commerce. As the largest moon, Tampa Quad boasts more inhabitants per square foot than any other, while still maintaining as much wild space as Tampa One.

DELEINE

Deleine was the newest planet to be terraformed, mainly so that workers could be close to the plethora of uranium, iridium, and bauxite mines there. The extensive mining has caused health issues, especially among the less genetically diverse Socialites.

2127

CPSIA information can be obtained at www.ICGtesting.com
Printed in the USA
BVOW08s0840190616

452143BV00015B/62/P

9 781935 738794